S0-FBS-519

ACCLAIM FOR AARON PATTERSON

AIREL

"Move over, Twilight. Here comes Aaron Patterson."

—*Joshua Graham, bestselling author*
of Beyond Justice and Darkroom

"I was surprised by how much I really, really liked this book. I have not jumped on the whole 'fallen angel' bandwagon, just as I didn't jump on all of the vampire stories that came out after Twilight. This is not your typical fallen angel story. It is one that has left me breathlessly waiting for the next one in the series. Hurry up, please..."

—*Sandra Stiles*

"It takes rare talent for a man to write a novel from a male POV and have it published to great critical and commercial acclaim. But it takes a miracle for that same male—or in this case, males—to write a novel from the POV of a teenage girl and have it turn out as incredibly as did the new StoneHouse YA by Aaron Patterson and Chris White, Airel. From the first sentence, I felt compelled to dive into this young woman's story and just as importantly, I felt like I personally knew her, which means I laughed, stressed, and cried right along with her. A beautifully written and crafted fiction about teenage innocence, faith, loss, and love. A must read for teens and adults alike."

—*Vincent Zandri, International Bestselling Author*
of The Remains, The Innocent, and Concrete Pearl

"An amazing story that will captivate audiences ranging from young adult to the young at heart. Airel crosses boundaries in a fascinating and unforgettable way to engage readers within a story that will not soon be forgotten."

—*Amazon Reviewer*

"I am happy to say that this novel is one of my favorites of its kind. I never thought I could read a novel like this and be so swept away. I am always willing to try new books, but I usually steer clear of this kind of novel. Not anymore. Not when I can be so engrossed into the character's story, like I was with the beautiful Airel, that before I know it, it's over. I kept turning the pages, wanting to—no, NEEDING to—know what was going to happen next."

—*Molly Edwards, Willow Spring, NC*

"The word 'enjoyed' somehow doesn't express how much, in a positive light, what this book The Airel Saga, Book 1 gave me. I loved the book and can hardly wait for the sequel. Though the story line is about Airel's teenage experience, I, at 75, truly enjoyed the read and was able to identify with her: As it happened to Airel, I felt it was happening to me."

—Amazon Reviewer

ACCLAIM FOR CHRIS WHITE

THE MARSBURG DIARY

"Yikes. This is one well-written and very strange book which will pique your interest from beginning to end. The author does a masterful job of moving you between centuries as you read two different point-of-view stories about one very unusual book. The telling of the tale, as found in the father's diary from the 1800s, is very well portrayed, and the writer has you believing you are actually back in that time period. Stepping forward to today, you experience the son's horror as he reads both his father's diary and the unusual book, and discovers it is currently driving him into the same mindset it created in his father ... near insanity. This is one roller coaster of a read and is sure to delight fans of the occult, supernatural occurrences, and mystery. A solid 4 1/2 star read."

—POIA, top Amazon reviewer

"A story that conjures mystery, suspense, and dark evils, THE MARSBURG DIARY is a page turner. White calls on the spirit of Steven King, Jules Verne, and Edgar Allen Poe to create a contemporary story that is as compelling as it is enduring. Marsburg learns of his father's past through a diary, a past filled with horror and mystery. But history doesn't stay in the past and visits Marsburg, sending him into his own thrilling adventures. THE MARSBURG DIARY is to AIREL what Torchwood is to Doctor Who: a grownup, stay-up-late, dark theme on a masterful series."

—Peter Leavell, Meridian, ID

"I really love Chris White's writing. He's extremely talented, and he is quickly becoming a favorite of mine."

—Michelle Vasquez, Life in Review

K: [PHANTASMAGORIA]

"Chris White has the talent of long-ago writers interlaced with his own unique voice. Anything this man writes keeps me up. I literally have to schedule time to read his work because I know when I start I'll not eat, sleep, or bathe until I've finished it. K: [PHANTASMAGORIA] is nothing short of his signature work. In fact, this might be his best novel to date. K is a character that you can't even begin to summarize. His experiences are all too familiar on so many levels. His relationship with others and God is eerily too close to home for not only myself, but so many I know. You simply have to read this book."

—*Bri Clark, Meridian, ID*

MORGANTOWN PUBLIC LIBRARY
373 SPRUCE STREET
MORGANTOWN, WV 26505

URIEL

THE PRICE

Book 6, Part 11-12

Aaron Patterson

Chris White

MORGANTOWN PUBLIC LIBRARY
373 SPRUCE STREET
MORGANTOWN, WV 26505

Copyright ©2010, 2011, 2012, 2013 by Aaron Patterson and Chris White

All rights reserved as permitted under the U.S. Copyright Act of 1976. No part of this publication may be reproduced, distributed, or transmitted in any form or by any means, or stored in a database or retrieval system, without the prior permission of the publisher.

StoneHouse Ink 2013
StoneHouse Ink
Boise, ID 83713
http://www.stonehouseink.net

First eBook Edition: 2013
First Paperback Edition 2013

ISBN: 978-1-62482-111-0

The characters and events portrayed in this book are fictitious. Any similarity to a real person, living or dead, is coincidental and not intended by the author.

Uriel: a novel/by Aaron Patterson & Chris White

Cover design by © Claudia McKinney - phatpuppyart.com
Layout design by Ross Burck – rossburck@gmail.com

Published in the United States of America

StoneHouse Ink

Also by Aaron Patterson

Sweet Dreams (Book 1)
Dream On (Book 2)
In Your Dreams (Book 3)
Breaking Steele
Twisting Steele
Melting Steele
Airel (Book 1)
Airel (Book 2)
Michael (Book 3)
Michael (Book 4)
Uriel (Book 5)
Uriel (Book 6)
19 (Digital Short)
The Craigslist Killer (Digital Short)
Zombie High (Digital Short)
Elena's Secret: A Vampire Diaries story

Also by Chris White

Airel (Book 1)
Airel (Book 2)
Michael (Book 3)
Michael (Book 4)
Uriel (Book 5)
Uriel (Book 6)
The Marsburg Diary (Book 1, Airel Saga novellas)
The Wagner Diary (Book 2, Airel Saga novellas)
The Falkenhayn Diary (Book 3, Airel Saga novellas)
The Great Jammy Adventure of the Flying Cowboy (a children's book)
Strongbox (a digital short)
Amethyst (a digital short)

PART ELEVEN

THE PRICE

CHAPTER I

Boise, Idaho, Present Day

AIREL LAY STILL. DEATHLY still. Dirk Elliott bent to her chest and laid an ear over her heart, listening for the sounds of life as they faded.

Then it beat no more. Dirk picked Airel up and carried her body into the women's restroom, depositing her on the toilet in the far stall. He left the door open wide. He felt like bragging about his latest conquest.

He stood at the door to the stall and stared at her. Airel was strong, much stronger than he ever imagined. He could feel her—he possessed every one of her thoughts, emotions, and fears now. She was a walking contradiction too, as much human as angel.

Leaving the bathroom, he went to the table where she had been reading. He sat and picked up his book, Tennyson, and picked up where he'd left off. Airel was no more . . . but that didn't mean he had to stop reading right when it was beginning to get good.

A few minutes later, a scream came from the bathroom and a hysterical woman ran out, gasping, "She's dead. She's dead." Dirk smirked and continued reading. After a few more minutes, the library was abuzz with activity.

Standing, he walked out the front doors, calm. Sirens in the distance made him chuckle. This would be on the news. Everyone would talk, but he wouldn't stay to feed on the chaos. He had a few loose ends to tie up; he had a fee to collect and a pet to feed.

"Rest well, Airel," he said. "Maybe in another life we could have been . . . something . . . but as it stands, we can only play the parts we were born to play."

He would not miss her—not really. She was a part of him now, and in some cheesy, romantic way, they would be together forever, wouldn't they? He laughed out loud. Well . . . it was a nice thought, anyway.

I COULD FEEL DIRK kissing me and for a moment, I kissed him back, pulling him into me hard, letting out all my pent-up emotions. Michael was the furthest thing from my mind and what I was doing didn't matter—not anymore.

But then something died out of me and I was abandoned. The light couldn't reach me. I was underwater.

My head spun. I opened my eyes, and then I saw my attacker beyond the Dirk-mask he wore. It was a child, a boy of about ten. His face was all malice, pure murder, and the way it looked frightened me more than I'd ever been. I pulled back and tried to break away, but my limbs wouldn't work. I could hear him feeding on me; I could hear him sucking, gorging on my heart, my soul. He said, "Calm yourself, Airel. Give over to me, and you will have the rest you desire."

She was screaming at me, but her voice made no sense. She was drowning in a sea of nothing far away.

My instincts kicked in and I called for the Sword.

Nothing happened.

I raged, kicked to launch into flight, swearing to rip his head from his slimy little body.

Nothing.

It was all inside my head—a dream. Nothing was possible.

Memories of my childhood bubbled up and came to the surface. My first puppy, Max. He was so cute and got into everything. My dad would find his shoes chewed up and yell at me. The huge swing at the park behind the SuperMart. Mom would push me so high. The higher I went, the more I would giggle. She was so kind to me, and now . . .

She kept screaming something. What was she yelling? I was only sleeping. Why was She all worked up? Why?

"Defend—protect your mind, Airel!"

Kim. The first time we met. She was so hyper, always the one making lame jokes and laughing at them no matter what anyone else thought. I missed her. Lazy Sundays watching old movies, building pillow forts, playing dress up and stealing Mom's makeup.

"Defend!"

Why was I so tired? How can I be tired? I'm already sleeping.

Ice cream with Dad after our daddy/daughter dates. He would listen to me, hold the door open, and tell me I was his favorite daughter. I would laugh. "Dad, I'm your only daughter." But then he would get this far-off look, a look I saw more and more these days. The one that seemed to say, "I shouldn't be your father; you shouldn't be here." Why did he not want me? It was like I was something instead of someone.

"Fight back, Airel!"

Michael and his kiss, the way his arms felt around me, how he protected me from so much evil in the world. His kindness, how he made me feel . . . I was so happy when I was with him. But where was he? Why was I kissing Dirk?

"Airel!"

Dirk stood over me, taking from me all I treasured--my memories, my life. Reality crashed through my numbness and then I knew I couldn't fight back, not physically. My body was as good as dead, and I knew too well how that felt.

I walled up inside the tiniest part of my soul, the dwelling place of my hopes and dreams. There was rushing wind; there was suffocating water. I closed the door on the world and I slept.

MICHAEL ALEXANDER STOOD OVER Airel and wept.

Tubes ran down her nose and throat. Her skin was pallid gray—even her hair was dull and mousy. He took her hand and held it up to his lips, kissing it. She was cold and lifeless.

He remembered their last conversation.

More tears ran down his cheeks. His chest was tight—it hurt all the way through to his spine. He couldn't breathe. With her dad away on business, her mom sat alone by the bedside, an empty woman in a plastic chair with the full distance of life's race in her eyes. She did not acknowledge Michael. She didn't acknowledge anyone.

Ellie spoke softly to him. "How are you holding up?"

Michael shook his head. There were no words for it.

Ellie coughed, sounding sick. He turned to her and noticed she seemed ill. She turned up a corner of her mouth and reached for him, drawing him in, hugging him. He let her. She was his last friend right now, one of the only people who knew the whole story. She knew what he was and who he might become. "You fight it,

Michael. Don't let them win, you hear me? Don't you give up on her, and don't give up on yourself, Michael Alexander." She held his face in her hands and smiled again. "Fight. I mean it."

How she knew what he'd been going through, he couldn't say. Nodding, he gave her one more sidearm hug and wiped his eyes with the back of his hand. "They say it's a coma. She could wake up anytime. Or never." His voice cracked, but he swallowed the doubt away again and shoved his hands into his pockets.

Ellie rubbed her arm and winced. Michael took another look at her. "Are you okay?"

She sighed. "No." She glanced at Airel's mom and lowered her voice. "Can we talk?" She ticked her head toward the hall.

Michael followed her out.

Ellie rolled up her shirtsleeve. Black webs twisted up and down her arm. Michael knew what it was, but he caught his breath anyway. He'd been fighting the same thing. "When did it start?"

Ellie kept her eyes locked on her arm and shrugged. "A few days ago. It's spreading."

Michael cursed and clenched his fists so hard that his knuckles turned white. "It's my fault. You shouldn't have taken it from me."

Ellie rubbed her eyes with the heels of her hands. "Michael, it was the only choice left and you know it."

"Yeah, but it didn't work. Look at you, Ellie."

"Hey, do I seem worried to you?"

"Does Kreios know?"

She exhaled. "He helped me once before."

"Something's different this time, Ellie." Michael didn't want to say it out loud. It possessed its own intelligence—it seemed to be alive, to think, to reason. It was stronger, more invasive. "I'm not sure I can do this anymore."

He felt her hand grasp his arm. "Don't you say things like that, mate. I'll not have you giving up."

He breathed; it was jagged. "I don't have the Mark on my body, Ellie. It's in my mind. It's there—I can feel it. The Bloodstone is calling me." Their eyes met, and the full weight of this truth passed between them. "I'm the rightful heir in the Alexander line. If I don't obey, it will try to kill me."

Ellie rolled her sleeve down and seemed to be considering what he said. "This isn't in any of the old Books. I'm at a loss, mate. All I know is that something's moving, a war's coming . . . and you're at the center of it. My dreams are never wrong. I still believe you can choose; you have free will, Michael."

"Choosing between two different kinds of sure death doesn't feel like much of a choice."

Ellie shrugged. She pointed back into Airel's room. "What about her? Was she ready? Did she have enough choices? Enough time to make them?"

"I've messed things up with her." He fought back tears. "I hear it calling to me; I can't stop the voices in my head. I feel like I'm going crazy."

Ellie took him by the shoulders—she was strong. Mist rolled off her, a dark fog. "You have to destroy it, Michael. Destroy the Bloodstone. It will never stop—surely you know this. The only one who can destroy it is the rightful Seer—you. I can't tell you how to do it, but I know the Brotherhood inside and out, and so do you." She pointed toward Airel's hollow body, kept alive by machines. "You do whatever it takes, do whatever you must—become the Seer, for all I care. But once you do, take that cursed thing and destroy it."

Tears. "I can't."

"Did you hear what I just said?"

"It will consume me. It will take over—it will control my every thought, my every action."

"If that's the price, you must pay it. You're the only one who can, Michael. Like you said, you don't have much of a choice."

CHAPTER II

Boise, Idaho, Present Day

JOHN CROSS WAS TIRED. His daughter was in a coma, on life support, unable to breathe on her own, and his wife was wilting away. She couldn't be budged from Airel's bedside. It had only been a week and she was already down ten pounds. Ten pounds she couldn't afford to lose.

Tonight he wanted nothing more than to sit in his living room and watch the late-night newscast. But two minutes into it, the power went out. He cursed under his breath. Every light and appliance in the house was dead. It didn't take much investigation past a quick glance at the clock on the stove and the display on the thermostat. All dead.

He peeked out the back windows toward his neighbors. Their houses were dark too. He looked over his shoulder through the living room toward the front of the house. The streetlights weren't even on. "Big power outage."

He walked outside onto the front porch to survey the neighborhood. It was lifeless, quiet. That eerie quality was broken by the opening and shutting of a door about a block away, a conversation spilling out from the private parts of another house in the opposite direction. People were being driven outside by the cutoff.

John chuckled. Figures. The only time we ever engage our neighbors anymore is when something's gone wrong.

He heard the sound of breaking glass. He wheeled around. It had come from behind him, inside the house. His instincts to defend kicked in.

He hurried inside, hugging the wall, staying low, using to his advantage the training and experience he had acquired in his time as a weapon's smuggler. As he surveyed his house, clearing it step by step, room by room, his mind was on one thing—his study. Behind the bookcase was his gun safe, his weapon's cache.

He cleared the living room, the kitchen and dining room, but they were basically one space, and he cleared them at a glance. There was no evidence of ingress here—no broken glass. He, or they, have to be somewhere else. Maybe down the hall. Toward the study. John cursed, his back to the corner of the wall that adjoined the hallway that led to his office. He got low and peeked around the corner.

Nothing.

He crept toward his study, but the door to the little half bath came first. He had to clear that room before moving past it. With the overwhelming feeling that it might be his last act on earth, and as quietly as possible, he pushed the partially open door wide, flicking on the light switch.

Nothing happened.

I forgot—the power's out.

For a moment, John's heart stopped, the hand of terror wrapping fully around it as he fumbled in the darkness. But his eyes adjusted and he perceived that the little room was empty. He breathed in hard and his heart pounded in his ears.

He turned toward his study, giving a slight shiver, so close to the security granted by the explosive power of his weapons. The study was empty—no intruder. He was beginning to wonder if this was all in his mind, if there had been anyone at all.

John swung the bookcase open and began working the combination to the safe. There was a 12-gauge Mossberg in there with six shells of birdshot in the magazine. That'll talk to 'em. He grabbed some rifled slugs and jammed them into his pockets.

He didn't have much time to think. He only had enough time to rack the slide on the Mossberg, jacking a shell into the chamber. Before he could take it off safety, before he could turn around, he was dropped to his knees by a blow to his leg that crackled through him in a blaze of pain. He cried out. It took all he had to keep the shotgun under control as he fell.

"How does it feel, Cross?" came the shrill voice of his attacker.

John tried to breathe through the pain that was even now ebbing away. "Ow. Not good," he groaned, "if you really must know." His right thigh was on fire. John suspected it had been a baseball bat swung at his leg. As he turned to face his attacker, his suspicions were confirmed.

"Don't get cute," the assailant said, letting the wooden bat fall to the carpeted floor, standing over him with a pistol aimed point-blank at his head. "Drop it."

John looked at him. "What, this old thing?" he asked, cocking his head at the shotgun in his hands. John had managed to get himself turned around into a sitting position with the barrel of the shotgun pointing vaguely upward at the ceiling and slightly forward to where the intruder, who he could now see was wearing a mask, stood over him. John's right hand was still in place by the trigger, though his left had been used to support his weight as he turned around to face his enemy.

"Would you like to die?" the man asked. "Drop your gun."

The implication of the question was that he had something for which he wanted to live. John's brow furrowed as his right thumb worked against the safety release on the shotgun. But he wasn't sure anymore. His life was nothing but pain and questions. "Are you trying to piss me off?"

The shrill voice of the thug rose in pitch and volume. "I said, do you want to die?" He cocked the hammer on the revolver and John watched the cylinder rotate into position, readying the shot from the bullet that might take his life.

John's shotgun finally snicked quietly into fire mode, and as it did, his grip changed. His forefinger and middle finger gripped the weapon in front of the trigger guard and his ring finger slipped smoothly over the trigger, his thumb wrapping around the receiver. The butt stock was wedged firmly against the carpet at the baseboard. He applied more pressure with his ring finger. "Are you working for MAGICIAN, or are you just some poor slob who's trying to rob the wrong house?"

"Shut up! Drop your weapon and tell me where it is!"

"If you were going to kill me, I'd be dead already. As for what you want, I don't have it. Or didn't you get the memo?" Trigger pressure increased slowly and steadily. "Amateur." The trigger clicked against the release pawl, and the shotgun's firing pin slammed home against the primer at the base of the shell in the chamber. But there was only an audible click.

Dud, John thought, along with a few other choice words.

As the consequences of this unforeseen event ran wild in his mind, he saw raw surprise scatter across the thug's eyes like scared children running from a terrifying dog. Yeah, he didn't expect I'd fire. Now he's just cheated death and he's not sure what to do about it. Maybe they didn't come to kill me.

The thug had been standing close—too close—with his right foot placed between both of John's, the muzzle of the pistol extended to within a foot of John's forehead. He thinks he can't miss from this distance.

John twisted sharply to his left, ducking down and away from the revolver, sweeping his left foot across the carpet toward the thug's right foot. As he did this, he kicked upward toward the knee with his right. When the blow landed, he could hear a low, snapping thud as the attacker's knee dislocated.

The man went down with a startled cry, but he held fast to the pistol. As he grasped it, he squeezed the trigger and dropped the hammer. The revolver spat harshly, roaring into the wall just above John's head.

The Mossberg was still in John's right hand, its barrel now lying across his injured thigh, angling lower than before, but still pointing over the head of the attacker.

It was coming down to this—the strong would survive. That was true for John Cross in every aspect of life right now.

The thug was moaning before him on the floor, not an arm's length away, curled up and clutching at his knee. John reached out with his left hand and grasped the shotgun by the forend, freeing his right hand for other work. He punched the man in the throat, softening him completely now. He was a puddle of goo and choking tears.

John relieved the man of the revolver, tossed it aside, and got to his feet. He stood over him and aimed the muzzle of the shotgun at his head, point-blank. "Are you leaving now, or were you hoping for a wild second chance?" He began to reach down to unmask the villain when the shotgun finally went off.

It wasn't a dud—it was a hangfire.

There was nothing left of the man's mask now, or his head. This was disturbing, to be sure, and not least because of the mess it had produced in John's study. But none of that disturbed him as much as did the thought that this seemingly amateur thug had known his name. How does it feel, Cross? The words echoed in John's mind.

He scratched his temple with the muzzle of the shotgun. It was warm. I need to clear the rest of the house. There might be another. He racked the slide and proceeded into the hallway.

CHAPTER III

Sawtooth Mountains of Idaho, Present Day

ELLIE LAY SHIVERING UNDER several blankets in the library before the fire. She was not well, not at all. She felt fatigued at all times lately. She lacked the strength to do much of anything for herself. Even getting up to use the loo was a trial. She had been camped out on the couch in the library by the never-ending fire for the past week, and she couldn't get warm.

She pored over books searching for an answer, something to tell her what Michael could do, if there was a way to destroy the Bloodstone and who John Cross really was. She was about to give up when she came across a marriage license through an online tracking service. Airel's birth certificate, documents from the hospital, and even vaccination records—it was all there, everything but what happened before Mr. and Mrs. Cross were married.

This aborted paper trail concerned Ellie. Everyone left a mark. She knew this because she was so good at leaving just the right amount of information in her wake. If anyone looked into her, they would see enough to satisfy their curiosity, but John Cross was invisible. It was all too clean.

One of her hobbies was hacking. Her years of experience made her elite. She remembered when the Web had first launched, how she was one of the first to realize its true potential. Now like a bloodhound on a scent, she dug into the national database for missing persons and hacked through CIA and FBI firewalls—and not just those, but the shadow companies who served them—to see if there was anyone matching John Cross's profile who had gone missing or been found. She limited her search to the twenty-year span before John had married his wife.

There were a few thousand John Does missing within that time frame and a few hundred found. But all of these records were either hard copy or microfiche and not available online. She did learn that John Cross worked freelance for the CIA off and on. What kind of man freelances for the CI-freaking-A?

He owned a company—"Revolutionary Technologies, LLC"— and used it to move tech like weapons and guidance chips. If a "sensitive" piece of equipment needed to get from point A to point B, it seemed John Cross was your man. But like most entrepreneurs untrained and unchecked by the Company—the CIA—he was a risk. He could always cut and run. The CIA didn't like loose ends, and John Cross was potentially a big one. So, Johnny boy. What have they got on you that's keeping you in line? She wondered if it had an expiration date and how desperate that might make him.

Ellie could see now why he was so secretive. But that didn't explain his empty past.

She shut her laptop and stood with great effort.

"You are not well," Kreios said. He was standing by the fire, quietly watching her.

"You scared me." She wore long sleeves to hide the Mark, but he could read her thoughts. So what's the point in hiding it from him? "The Mark is back, Father. I fear it has bonded to me in ways beyond what we first imagined."

Kreios did not betray any surprise. "When I took it from you, I saw that what I was taking bore Michael's signature. Of all people. It was noble of you to try to save one of them."

"Yes, well. I have much to pay for."

"Something distinct remained, though, something old. It was too entangled within you for me to try to remove it. I might have killed you."

Ellie thought of her past and the Bloodstone that consumed her, the one that also took her son from her. "That wasn't the first time I'd been marked."

"I know. That became clear over time."

"I'm sorry, Father. So many times, I . . . I wanted to come to you. I wanted to explain everything." She sat back down, exhausted.

"A father bears his burdens."

"I guess some sins are never forgiven," she said.

Kreios folded his arms across his chest. "Sins can be forgiven, but scars remain. And neither is forgotten."

Ellie knew that if she stayed, she would die a slow death—it would be painful. She had little time left to her. She wanted to be of further use before it was too late. "I have somewhere to be."

"Other than in your father's house?"

"And you have war on your mind."

Kreios shrugged. She could see his eyes darken to full black. "The world is thin, and yes, war is coming. You should stay here, daughter. Rest."

Now Ellie folded her arms. "I told you—I have large debts. I intend to pay them."

"With your life?"

"I spent my life racking them up. How else can they be paid?"

"You confuse your scars with your sins. They are not the same thing. You do not have to go."

"You know better than that, Father. I must go. Airel is slipping, Michael is fighting a battle he may very well lose, and you—you I can no longer read." She narrowed her eyes and concentrated as hard as she could on him. "No . . . no, darkness hides your mind from me."

He walked toward her, his eyes blazing. For the first time in her life, Ellie was scared of him. "I will not lose you again. You will stay. I am not asking."

"Nor am I." Ellie thought of the place she wanted to go and disappeared.

I COULD SEE MICHAEL crying, standing over my bed, looking at me as if I were already dead. I could hear him, see Mom sitting there trapped inside her own mind. But I couldn't move, couldn't express how I felt. My flesh was a prison.

The demon I now knew as Dirk Elliott thought I was dead. Or did he? Maybe he wants me alive, and he's going to come back for me.

Fear tore through me. I struggled to get back to my body, but nothing worked. Dirk had damaged me badly, maybe permanently. I was so tired. I dreamed, remembered, and wept for the life I might never experience. Michael was standing right there, but I would never get to tell him I was sorry, that I loved him.

Ellie said something to him and then they left the room. My heart broke. What if he never comes back? What if I don't?

CHAPTER IV

Arabia, 788 B.C.

URIEL HAD NO MEMORY of this state of being.

Then the perspective switched, and she hovered above herself. I am overtaken—possessed in every way—by the Bloodstone, by evil. The perspective switched again and she flew high above it all, watching what happened next.

At the center of her being was a flame. She understood it to be her heart, and just as she understood this, she watched as its light was snuffed.

But it didn't go out. It was merely redefined. What was once light and truth was now darkness and untruth. And there was a difference between untruth and lies, for lies were ultimately creative and therefore, subject to the kingdom of El. Untruth, however, was a simple opposite. And simple opposites were clean and free.

High above, observing, she knew all of that to be blatant fraud, but in her memories she could see how and why she bought it, believed it, why it had seemed sensible, even logical.

Her light became darkness. Therefore, her darkness became light. And now she was free from all restraint, all sense of remorse, guilt, fear, and doubt because there was no tomorrow, no eternity, nothing but what pleasure could be derived in the Now, the Self.

She lived for whim. She was like the wind.

And then—thirst. Hunger. She wanted only one thing. Destruction. The hatred she first felt when she was activated by the Brotherhood now came rolling back over her, a thousand thousand times stronger now, and she knew where she would go and what she would do.

Ke'elei would fall and at her hand.

Uriel was only slightly aware of herself as she swirled down and down, beneath the folds of the ground, entangled with the grasping fingers of the Bloodstone. She had no rest from its wickedness; there was no place to which she could run from him and be safe. Her mind was beginning to bend in unnatural ways now, and her thoughts were beginning to come from somewhere outside herself.

The dual presence moved deep below the City of Refuge and began to spread itself like a disease in the bedrock.

"NEVER LET IT BE said that our forces lack imagination," said Piankhy, the commander of the armies of the Brotherhood, his countenance lit in red by the presence of the Bloodstone. He brooded over its captivating lust-ridden beauty in the seclusion of his campaign tent on a little knoll in the wood a few leagues from Ke'elei.

This strategy, which he was just now beginning to understand, was new—it was unique.

The Brotherhood horde that had massed itself in its hundreds of thousands at the gates of Ke'elei was only one element of a two-pronged attack. The other element, the crushing blow, would come when the servants of El least expected it, and from impossible places.

Victory was assured. The Fallen, the angels who were not cursed, would become extinct today. This bitter feud would end and the true Nephilim would reign over the earth as it had been promised.

His Nubian armies had subdued the whole of Egypt, and like Alexander would hundreds of years later, Piankhy hungered for more. His mystic enthusiasms had led him to new depths, and his court magicians had uncovered new possibilities for conquest that made the natural world's wonders pale in comparison.

But it came at a price, for Piankhy would not be able to wallow in the selfsame glories as did the previous bearers of this precious stone. No, he would not be Seer. He would be forced to stand off at a distance as the Bloodstone moved and worked autonomously. He didn't understand all the details, but he did know that there was no room for an additional inhabitant now. There was already a confusion of presence in and around the Bloodstone, a duality that at times made things . . . difficult for him.

Most of that did not matter, for his hunger in regard to the cog set of war was great indeed. So he had folded his Nubian armies into the Brotherhood and made dark pacts with unseen forces under the cover of night. His power multiplied, and as they marched over deserts and high, wooded plains, terrorizing and pillaging as they went, the plan had been made clear in his mind.

He would lay siege to the City of Refuge and he would subdue the armies of the servants of El, this unknown god. Whether his armies were the main force today, or the diversion, was meaningless drivel. He would drive his forces over and through those walls, those gates, no matter what opposed him.

At the end of this day, Piankhy would own the victory; he would stand above all as the strongman.

He watched as the Bloodstone hovered over his open hands in space, lighting the interior of his tent in iniquitous red. It then dissolved into nothing with one clearly understood directive: "Begin." The Bloodstone had disappeared from sight.

He summoned his generals. Now he issued the order to advance.

YAMANU AND ZEDKIEL GLANCED at each other as they ran down the streets of Ke'elei, Veridon and a few other stout hearts at their sides. Yamanu knew—they all knew—time was short.

They were in full battle dress, their swords and breastplates gleaming, their massive shields grasped in the hand and strapped to the off-side forearm of each angel of El.

Lesser folk, even some who were not even half angelic, even full-blood men, who had come to the City of Refuge in years past dodged out of the way of this cohort of brave warriors as they ran up the high street toward the Circle of Elders.

They were seeking a final audience with Anael. Yamanu thought that perhaps he might be convinced, one last time, to see the imminent danger at hand and issue an order to fly from here. Yamanu thought he might be convinced—but he had little real hope for it.

The angelic cohort, with Yamanu and Veridon now at its head, spilled into the courtyard, the seats of the court encircled by those ancient Corinthian stone columns of purest white. The tall old oak at the north side had long ago withered and dried up, most of its smaller limbs having dropped and shattered upon the cobblestone floor below. "This is a place of death," Veridon said, breathing hard. Yamanu looked around them. "Anael!" he called out. "We seek an audience with the head of the council. Show yourself."

Zedkiel had joined them by now and began calling out as well. "Anael! Come forth. We command you in the name of El to fulfill your obligation to the people of Ke'elei." A serious glance passed between Zed and Yam. They trod on dangerous ground now.

A low cackle came from the direction of the great oak. An errant breeze lifted a white wisp like a flag, revealing the position of the ancient one. "You command me in the name of El? Sentimentalities."

The angels moved quickly toward the oak and surrounded Anael, who was reclined in the dirt amongst the great, gnarled roots. Veridon drew his sword and stepped forward. "Stand, Anael, and bear witness."

But Anael waved a finger and Veridon's sword was wrenched from his grip and cast away, clattering to the ground. "Stand aside, little boy, before you get hurt." He looked disgusted, as if a fly was pestering him. "Who is this that darkens the council's Circle with nonsense and folly?" Anael appeared to be very frail and aged, his face drawn with many lines. "Why are you young fools bothering me?"

"Anael," Yamanu said, "the whole of the Brotherhood horde armies are encamped at our very gates. We must fly, or we will all die this very day."

Anael cackled low for a long time, and then arched an eyebrow at him. "Then," he said, laughing, "you must go and fight." He cackled again. "I will never issue the order to fly."

Veridon roared at the wizened angel in fury. "Why will you not? Thousands will die if you do not! Never mind the loss of the city— we shall concede it. But if we do not fly, we will perish. All of us."

Anael shrugged. "But it would break the pact we've made." His eyes then turned malicious and red. "In good faith." His hands came up like claws and a burst of red power, like lightning, exploded from him, leveling the old tree and scattering the angels like twigs. When the dust had settled, Yamanu looked up to behold Anael hovering above the ground on a disc of red light, his hands upraised and grasping a staff of blood light, a lightning bolt that pulsed in red frenzy.

"You trusting sheep." Anael's voice echoed harshly off the cold stone of the mountains that surrounded the City of Refuge. "You awaken only now?" He laughed. "It has been too late for you for hundreds of years."

Yamanu stood to his feet, breathing hard, wondering what he could do to oppose this. He could think of nothing. This was something new under the sun, something he had not foreseen. El, he cried out within himself, what has happened? What new power is this which Anael wields against your servants?

"All you must do today," Anael said, "is die."

Then a great clashing sound came from the main gates, and the angels turned toward it. There was a shout, the war cry of a hundred thousand demon Brothers, coming from just outside the city walls.

Yamanu's eyes were wide with fear. "The final battle has begun."

CHAPTER V

Boise Idaho, Present Day

JOHN CLEARED THE GROUND level of his house quickly. He found no one and nothing, so he crept up the stairs, looking for enemies. It wasn't exactly fun, it wasn't what he might call enjoyable, and yet somehow he only really felt alive when his life was at stake. I guess that's what led me down this path in the first place. The typical version of the American dream just wasn't ever enough for me. I always knew there was more, as if I was meant to live a different life.

Voices resounded in his head, accusing voices that told him he never really loved his wife and daughter, not if he always felt the need to go off and play tough guy all over the world. Clearly he loved the job more than the home life, and it had shown in his actions. He wondered if he'd ever given them enough of himself. Would they say, now, that he had loved them with everything he had in him? Why do I feel like having a wife and a child was a mistake, as if I was going against my own convictions?

More voices piled up guilt and regret and shame, telling him the only thing that had ever satisfied him had been this, stalking killers and thugs, making illicit deals in dark alleyways with unscrupulous men, selling power to the power hungry. The fact was, he was hungry for power too. He was addicted to it.

He peeked into the guest room, gun first. Nothing. Nothing under the bed, nothing in the closet. He felt like he was going through the same motions, the same drill he used to perform for Airel when she was only five or six, checking the room for monsters. See, sweetheart? Nobody's in your closet. There are no bad men in this house.

What was it that drove him to pursue this life? Why had there been so much secrecy over the years? It was like his own family didn't even know him, not really. Why was he so driven toward risk, toward grappling with rough and monstrous men in dark places?

Maybe it's just in my blood—that's all.

Was that it? Was it something inevitable, something he had inherited?

As he came back into the hallway at the top of the stairs, his ears pricked. What is that? He couldn't place the noise he heard. He thought it was coming from Airel's room—the last place he wanted to find something, the last place he wanted to see—but he didn't know what the sound was. He shook his head and trying to get a clear thought through his brain. He double-checked that the safety was off on his 12-gauge and walked toward the source.

There it is again. It sounded like someone choking. John swallowed. The door to Airel's room was open a crack. He was sure he had left it closed. The light from the moon, so out of place in this powered-down electric suburbia, washed out into the hallway. Shadows moved in its beams. Somebody's in there.

John's pulse quickened to a thunderous gallop, nearly deafening him as it pounded through his ears. He stood six feet away from the door to his comatose daughter's bedroom, thinking of his next move. He brought the butt stock up and crooked it tightly into his shoulder. He looked down the barrel as he raised it, drawing a bead on the door at just below head height. He couldn't control his breathing; his aim was inconsistent, bobbing up and down. He laid a finger across the trigger. He was ready.

But he wasn't ready for this.

"Cross," came a hissing whisper from inside the room.

It chilled him right down to his toenails. He felt the great tug of fear pulling him backward palpably, urging him to flee. "Step out in the hallway, bastard," he said. "I've got something for you."

The door edged a little toward the jamb the way it would when there was a sudden differential of air pressure in the house, like when the heat kicked on. Movement. Shadows in the darkness. And a smell of rottenness.

"Come out!" John commanded.

The door, which opened inward toward the bedroom and which was not a cheap hollow core but rather a solid pine slab, now exploded through the jamb into the hallway, ripping off its hinges. The intruder followed immediately and he was a big boy, towering over John by at least a foot, maybe more. It was hard to see details in the dark.

He raised the muzzle of the Mossberg and squeezed the trigger. The muzzle flash revealed something impossible. It was all black, unclothed. Its mouth—such as it was—was full of fangs. And it had a tail. He saw all this in the blink of an eye. This wasn't a man. It was something straight from hell.

CHAPTER VI

Sawtooth Mountains of Idaho, Present Day

KREIOS AROSE, MILLIONS OF thoughts pouring through him. He felt as if he would run in mad circles until insanity finally took him, and then . . . what? El! Where is the end?

Ellie would not listen—no one would listen.

"All these books," he said, looking at the piles he had amassed, "and not a single answer." He shoved the stacks over, kicking the table legs, scattering things in all directions. He knew of her Mark, had spent days going over and over his books to find a way to save her. But there was nothing. Now she had left again and he had other matters to attend to, but his anger flowed through him and he left it unchecked.

Impulsively, he stalked to the door of his closet. The bare concrete room. The Threshold. He would not stand by and do nothing. His hand seized the doorknob and he wrenched it open without pause, keeping his eyes brazenly open. There was no need for him to focus any more intently than he already did upon the destination; he was of single purpose.

Cain.

The door did not show some otherworldly scene. It did not open upon the woods near where Cain had dwelt for so many thousands of years. It did not reveal the Keep of the Damned; it did not link to Sheol. It merely revealed a clean emptiness, a space much like the plain concrete room Kreios had built as a covering for this thin place.

And there was Cain, in the flesh, sitting on the floor. He bowed to the Angel of El, tucking his chin to his chest.

"Cain. It is time."

Cain looked him in the eyes.

"Release your dead upon the earth."

Cain hesitated. "What of the seal?"

"Release your dead, worm! Go forth! Do not spare. Kreios commands you."

A change came over the countenance of the man Cain, and his eyes dimmed to full pitch black. "It will be as you say." He did not issue another word, and in the next instant, he was taken away.

Kreios closed his eyes and quietly shut the door. He had not heard the command from El. He had not, as Cain had confirmed by his obvious question, been granted the authority to do as he had commanded him to do—the seal of which Cain had spoken was still intact.

This was not the time. But he had done it anyway, and now there was no stopping it. What Kreios had done was willfully out of order, and he knew it. His grief had mastered him, if only for a moment.

What will it cost?

He could feel it—the souls of the dead were rising through every thin place on the face of the earth. Would they now go forth? Would these who had unjustly killed before wage a just war upon the Brothers, those whose dark kingdom had enslaved them? Would

Cain fulfill his final purpose now?

Surely he would.

Surely.

CHAPTER VII

Sawtooth Mountains of Idaho, Present Day

MICHAEL FOUND THE HATCH to the tunnel leading to the place he once feared—the underground house Kreios built long ago, the place where he once fell in love with Airel, the place where he betrayed her, and the place where she died. It was a lifetime ago, as if a dream, yet coming back here seemed like the only thing to do.

"Hello?" he called to the empty room. A fire crackled in the hearth, indicating that someone had been here.

Thundering, Kreios flew into the room and pinned Michael to the wall a few feet off the floor. Michael was taken aback and Kreios glowed, white eyes flaming. "What do you want here, son of the damned?"

Michael struggled, but it was of no use. "I need your help . . . why are you so . . . ?"

Kreios lowered Michael and returned to his normal appearance. "Michael, I—" He took a few steps away and stared into the fire. It was dark outside, and snow was falling in huge, tumbling flakes.

"I talked with Ellie—"

Kreios spun around. "When? Why did you not stop her—where

is she?"

Michael held up his hands. "This was a couple of days ago, and no. I don't know where she is. I was hoping she was here."

"Continue."

It was Michael's turn to be angry. "Where were you? Airel is in a coma and you hide here? She needs you, Kreios, or did you forget that she's your granddaughter?"

Kreios lowered his head. "I should kill you for what you will become. But there are other matters . . ."

"No, there is Airel. No other matters, not the end of the world, not some stupid Bloodstone—only Airel. I'm leaving; I have no choice. Who will be here to make sure she's safe? Not you, apparently."

"She is safe enough. As long as she sleeps, no harm will come to her."

"And how do you know that? Some angel power or something?"

Kreios did not respond.

"That's what I thought."

"It calls to you Michael, does it not?"

Michael suddenly felt naked. The angel knows too much.

"You are growing weak. It is written all over you, boy." The angel snorted. "What will your decision be?"

Michael pretended not to be alarmed, but it was mostly for his own pride. If Kreios knew of his mental problems of late, there was no telling what else he might know. "I have an idea of how we might be able to destroy the Bloodstone, but I need your help."

Kreios dropped his hands. "Speak."

Elsewhere

IN MY DREAMS, I walked among the crumbling foundations of a building made of stone. It had been burned and was still smoking, its roof and doors—all those things that made it a place of safety— consumed and converted to smoke and ash and carried off to eternity by the winds. Most of its walls had been thrown down but some still stood, spaces for once-beautiful panes of colorful glass now empty, gaping open into the gray netherworld outside.

As I looked on, time revolved around me, and the ruins cooled and the floors in the building rotted and fell and decayed. From their detritus, from the ash of those fuels which had refused to fully burn but had instead fallen directly into the center of the building, I saw tender green shoots pushing up through the black ground.

The place felt vaguely familiar, but I didn't know why.

The sun pierced through a high round window that had been cut into the gable. There was no glass to restrict the life-giving warmth of this beam of sunshine. Like a fountain of life and warmth, it flowed down and around the leaves and stems and roots of the green shoots, caressing them and urging them upward into itself.

The walls were taller than I had first thought. The destruction was not as complete as I had imagined, and the building these foundations had been designed to hold could have been immense. If only . . .

Then I noticed an open space off to the side. There, resting against one wall, were large shards of mirror. They leaned at all angles, their reflections showing in one piece, the sun; in another, the gray skies; in another, the blackened stone of the walls. As I approached, most of them reflected bits of me.

I drew nearer and could plainly see that each reflection was different. Each one showed a different me—I was an infant with lots of dark brown hair, dozing in my father's arms. I was a little girl wearing a sundress in the kitchen with my mom and she was making jam, the smell tart and bright. I was a scared freshman walking to class on my first day of high school, hiding behind my long brown hair, my arms crossed over a thick American history text. I was the pariah who had just buried her best friend. I was the girlfriend of Michael Alexander.

Darkness stole in. There was subtraction, and I felt loss for the first time.

Looking around, I saw that the plants were there, but they were still. They had gone mostly dormant and dead brown. The sun hid itself above and beyond the clouds. The walls around me were dry and cracked; they looked as if they might topple over in a stiff breeze.

I suddenly understood why this place felt so familiar to me. This building is my life. And it was in ruins.

I looked back to the mirrors now, and the strangest thing was happening. The whole assembly began to rotate like a pinwheel in the wind, and I understood that each of these versions of me had fallen short of El's plan for my life. The pinwheel became a saw blade.

I began to gasp for air; I fell to my knees.

The spinning mirrors now started to rotate independently, a jagged kaleidoscope showing millions of versions of me, of Airel, the invisible girl, now reflected and on display as she truly was, no masks, no lies, and no illusions. Just me. Just me and everything I had done and missed in life. I felt like an utter failure.

Then the kaleidoscope sped up and became merged into one image: It was me—it wasn't me. It was like me—it wasn't like me. Perhaps I was like it—maybe that was more accurate. It was masculine, it was feminine, it was neither. It was a presence.

I was very still. I was filled with more fear than I had ever felt before; I was filled with joy to bursting. She?

"Stand."

I stood, slowly. "Who are you?"

"You already know."

I was silent, my mind flitting like a bird from one branch of thought to another—school crushes, funerals. Weddings, family trips, my first loose tooth. Relationship drama. Grades. Seasons. I realized that I was only one of many created beings for whom everything had slipped out of control. This happened to everyone. It was normal. Intentional. Part of the design. How could that be part of the plan? Isn't it imperfect? Flawed?

"Life under the sun is found in places like this, Airel. The flaws serve the truth by bearing witness to just how true Truth is. Mountains are mountains not just because of themselves, but because of the valleys that show their size, scope, and grandeur."

I soaked in this. "But I feel so inadequate. Like such a failure. If I could have had more time . . . I could have done more. I could have been more."

"You keep trying to do things alone, in your own power, but you miss the real strength. True power only comes by trusting in what is beyond you."

I began to weep. But why?

"Because I love you."

"Yes," I argued again, "but why?"

I felt She smile, and the sun shattered the clouds high above, spilling over me like water, cascading over every part of me, warming me. "I will never leave you. I love you just as you are, but I will not leave you that way."

CHAPTER VIII

Arabia, 788 B.C.

THE BROTHERHOOD FORCES WERE SLAMMING against the gates, against the walls; they were everywhere at once. The captain of the watch issued the call for every able body to come to the aid of the warriors at the walls, whether man, angel, or halfbreed.

Cries rang out across the gathering night as Yamanu and his cohort approached. He heard the captain on the wall below. "Brace the gate! They are bringing fire!"

Yamanu, Zedkiel, and Veridon wheeled in the air high above the action, and the scene below them was not encouraging. Demon Brothers harnessed to heavy siege works by iron chains pulled, straining to wheel them to the base of the walls. Of these, Yamanu could see that the horde had fashioned at least four ballistae, crossbows so huge that they could fire bolts the size of small trees. The first one had already launched the opening salvo, a beam of wood the breadth of a man's shoulders and five times his height, the tip of which had been honed to a point, slathered in bitumen, and set ablaze prior to release. It struck the wall beside the gate and held fast for a moment in the joint between several stones, burning and sending flames upward until it fell under its own weight. It rolled back and away, setting the scrub of the forest afire.

The next engine of war released its deadly projectile, this one striking the main gates. It caused them to shudder violently under its impact, its sharp tip piercing one of the cubit-thick assemblies of planks of which the gates had been built. The blazing bitumen went to work, and the gate began to burn.

More bolts flew as the angels descended from the air to the top of the wall. One more bolt struck the gate while two others flew wild and bounced off impotently.

Yamanu lit on the wall's fighting top, looking around. Already, the horde had erected their breaching ladders and was ascending. Why are they only in human form, and where are the demons? Some had reached the battlements and were beginning to squeeze in between the merlons onto the parapet walk. "Veridon, behind you!" Yamanu drew steel, pointing behind his friend and ally.

Veridon spun on his foe with the powerful mace, a spiked orb tethered by a chain to a rod of iron, dropping the foul man by smashing his brains into tiny bits. "Yamanu, we need a little help from your shadowing arts, old friend." Veridon moved toward the next intruder.

Yamanu nodded. "I am working on it," he said, running his sword through and killing the next unfortunate enemy to ascend onto the wall walk of the barbican, the gatehouse of the city. He felt at once the drain as the horde gained ground. This battle was going to be hard to win if they were all weakened by the draw of the Brotherhood and unable to fight. "Zedkiel," he called out, "how are the archers faring?"

Zed landed not far away, having come from checking in with the captain of the watch. He shook his head.

Not good. Yamanu took a moment to breathe and focus. How

could he turn back so many? He tried to manifest the fog around them, but it was like using a cold spark to try to ignite wet timber. Something is wrong. Yamanu remembered how, so many years ago, he and his Shadowers had been sold out to the former Seer, and he also remembered who was his prime suspect. Anael. This is treachery most vile. "Veridon! We must stand and fight them hand to hand. I cannot draw the shadow over us." He hacked a hand off as it reached through the embrasure in the wall beside him. "Something is wrong."

He turned away from the wall toward the heart of the city and beheld sweeping red pulses of lightning striking over it, drawing closer to his position. It was Anael. He was using black arts to destroy the city from the rear, while the main Brotherhood force crashed against the wall upon which he stood.

Kreios, we could use a little help here. I hope you have not abandoned us utterly.

KREOIS WAS ALREADY ON his way, streaking across a high black sky above the atmosphere from halfway around the globe. He had sensed imminent danger for quite some time. Only now had his sense of duty finally outweighed the reluctance he had long felt toward his kin.

As he accelerated by a magnitude of ten past the speed of sound, his thoughts turned terrible. If Ke'elei has indeed become a target, I fear the worst. There can be no allies left to us if this is true. Only a handful of true warriors can remain. Yamanu and Zedkiel flashed into his mind, their faces anxious and dark.

URIEL FELT HERSELF BEING spun off, shunted. As she was
gathered together into what was once herself, she realized that she
wasn't the one in control anymore. Some other force from within
was in control of her. All her particles dangled from strings, which
made her dance on a lurid stage. The Bloodstone.

Part of her became fully manifest above ground and part of her
remained dispersed underground. On the city wall near the barbican,
she was humanoid, wearing a black cloak made of shadows, her
shadowing power drawing from and being augmented by her
angelic foes, even Yamanu. Beneath the ground, she was infiltrating
the soil, soaking her every molecule into the bedrock, the shale, the
granite on which the city of Ke'elei rested. Above, on the wall, she
advanced on the enemy, dagger in her right hand. Below, she spread
herself as thinly as possible over many square leagues past the
limits of the city.

Below ground, she waited.

Above ground, she attacked.

Veridon came first. Out of the blackness, she came from
behind—he never saw her. The blade of her dagger flashed out
against him, striking quick and low, slicing deep into the thigh,
severing the femoral artery. He did not cry out, but he did fall fast,
the mace he so skillfully wielded clattering to an awkward stop on
the pavements.

As he fell to one knee and wheeled around, searching for his
attacker, she circled and advanced upon him again from his blind
side. The blood was already beginning to pool at his feet, pouring
from the artery she had sliced clean open. As she approached the
angel Veridon, she watched his body language. He fell slightly
forward into a slump, and she could tell that he knew he was dead.

But I'm not finished with you. Not yet.

She moved quickly in the darkness. Her left hand swept around his head and pulled it backward as her right moved in a flourish, a slicing circle that struck at his exposed neck. She melted back into the shadows before a single drop of blood could stain her. Her back to the wall of the keep, she observed calmly as Veridon began to drown in his own blood.

Next.

KREIOS REACHED OUT IN his mind and heart, looking for the captain of the watch, looking for anyone, looking for Veridon. Although he was drawing near to the City of Refuge, he still could not make contact with any of the thoughts of the angelic remnant. This worried him, and he was not prone to worry.

A burst of blackness then came up out of the ground from beneath him, and he narrowly missed a collision with it by virtue of the speed he was carrying. More dark shapes rose upward toward him. *I am getting closer.* He marveled at the size of the enemy army. *The Brotherhood means business this time.* More morbid sectors within his brain began to sound off in alarm that Ke'elei couldn't help but fall.

"Yamanu. Zedkiel." Kreios spoke their names into the air as he slowed, the city wall below and before him. "Where are you?"

The scene displayed before him was not encouraging. Brotherhood soldiers walked the battlements of the city wall freely, their hateful swaggering in this place like blasphemy.

The sky was red with the ominous light of the Bloodstone. It hovered over the action like a watchful eye, seeing everything. Then there came a furious, ugly blast of battle horns and the attack changed. The men charged, yelling, and the sound of tearing flesh broke through their battle cry. Wings filled and demons roared as they broke free of their brothers.

"Grant us mercy, El."

The already massive horde instantly doubled in size, blackening the air with their wings. There was no light, no cry from the angels, no horn of El sounding commands. There was only death and the screams of the dying.

BENEATH THE GROUND, URIEL began to convulse. The Bloodstone was manipulating her, forcing her to do things with her gift that she would never do of her own volition. She didn't want this anymore, yet she also found it to be irresistible.

As she convulsed, the bedrock began to vibrate and split upon its seams. Granite, veins of quartz and gold and coal and diamond, began to crack and move apart. Into these new cracks, she invaded as light pierces shadow. It behaved like light, but it was in fact darkness, and it spread itself into each void like the invisible radiations of the sun. As she worked herself in deeper, more cracks were precipitated, and than more.

The bedrock was becoming very unstable.

ABOVE GROUND, URIEL MOVED swiftly toward the angel Zedkiel. He was engaged with a large tusked demon Brother in a contest of swordsmanship. She watched and waited for an opening. It presented itself immediately.

Zedkiel faced away from her. As he crouched to his right to avoid a sweeping strike from his enemy, he prepared his blade for an unthrusting counterstrike in the wake of the demon's movement.

When he stood and extended his blade, his ribs were exposed all along his right side.

She struck quickly with the dagger, stabbing deeply between his ribs into his torso, burying it to the hilt. She left it embedded there and spun away, observing the effects.

Zedkiel cried out in pain, reaching instinctively across his body toward the wound. The tip of the blade had no doubt pierced his heart, for he then froze in anguish and shock. He became a motionless target.

The demon Brother seized the opportunity and took the angel's head off.

Uriel stepped forward to the headless corpse. Leaving the dagger behind, she removed Zedkiel's sword from his hand and took it as her own. Now she would finish Yamanu.

CHAPTER IX

Boise Idaho, Present Day

THE SHOTGUN BLAST SHOULD have killed the thing.
12-gauge, point-blank to the face. But it seemed like all it did
was make it angry. John let off a little emotional steam with a
blasphemous curse. He pumped the slide, jacking another shell into
the chamber.

The beast hissed, "I know your name. But do you?" It roared,
slamming a fist the size of a football through the wall. "Do you,
Derackson?"

John squeezed off another shot in the darkness at where he
supposed its face to be and then backed away. It had little effect, so
he pumped the slide again and took aim. "Wrong house, idiot. Who
is Derackson? What are you?"

Laughter. "You are afraid. Good," it said. Its voice was like
listening to swine rooting through rotting scraps. Each time the tail
of the thing collided with the walls or the ceiling, the frame of the
house shook.

Then another, smaller, slithered from the darkness and flapped
its wings, hissing. "We are not lost. We know what we were sent

here to do."

John lowered the muzzle, jabbed forward with it as if it were a sword, and unloaded the chamber into the beast's midsection.

Now this produced a result.

It fell away from him but only for an instant. It made a grab for the gun as it fell backward, but John managed to hang on to it.

He backed away again, racking the slide once more. He wasn't sure how many shells remained in the mag; he had lost count. He was down to his last one—maybe two—shells. The beast was gathering itself together for a lunge; it was renewing the attack. John decided he'd better burn another one, even if it was his last. I'll go down fighting you, whatever in hell you are. And when I'm out of ammo, I'm going to bash your ugly fangs in with the butt stock.

The fountain of fire that issued forth from the Mossberg, illuminating the scene, now only served to compound John's fears. He really was not hallucinating. He was actually battling with what looked like a freaking carnivorous dinosaur, and there were two of them, real-life black dragons in his own house, for crying out loud.

But he had injured the bigger one, and it went down hard this time. He racked the slide once more and heard his last shell slide into the chamber. He stepped toward the small one and shot it in the face. With a shriek, it flopped down like a fish and John barely managed to get out of the way of its tail. And than it was gone, crashing down the stairs, screeching like a wounded cat.

The big one languished on the floor, a dark shape that writhed in agony, hissing and spitting at him in rage.

John couldn't see much of anything, but he aimed for dead center mass because of how effective the shots he had taken there had been. "What are you? What do you want from me?"

The beast's laughter broke him from his reverie. Its movements began to slow. "You do not know, Derackson? How can you not know?" It growled out a curse and dug its claws into the floor.

"You die now!" John yelled. He thrust the muzzle forward, angry that this thing could find anything to laugh about at this moment. "Why are you laughing at me?"

"It is in your blood." It gagged in the dark, probably choking on its own bodily fluids. "You were thinking right. It's in your blood."

John was horrified. Did this thing read my mind? He clamped his jaw shut in rage and, furious, yanked on the trigger one last time.

In the aftermath of the explosion, all was finally still. He had overcome the monster. His ears were ringing and he was drenched in his own sweat. As his system dumped excess adrenaline into his bloodstream, he began to shake violently.

There in the hallway of his house, right outside his daughter's bedroom door, in a cloud of cordite, among fumes that reeked of rotten egg, he crumpled to the floor and began to weep.

And than the power came back on.

When his eyes had adjusted to the brightness, he practically leaped out of his skin trying to get away from what he saw. The house was quiet, but he forced himself to go after the other one.

He had to make sure it was dead. No rest for the wicked.

Elsewhere

I CAME BACK TO myself in a high meadow surrounded by wildflowers. At first, I didn't recognize where I was.

There was a great ring in the wild grass, a path made by walking. That much I recognized from dreams I'd had. But I didn't recognize what I saw next.

At the center of the ring stood a beautiful complex of buildings, all of them brand new and gleaming under silvery tiled roofs, the walls made of white stones that were a little translucent, a little luminescent.

I entered the buildings and explored them for what felt like sometimes, and then I came upon a great big open room. It was an atrium closed in by a dome of crystal glass at least a hundred feet across and three stories tall. The sun poured in through it and ran wild over ferns and shrubs and trees. Hummingbirds flitted from flower to flower, and as I looked up, smiling, I saw it.

The round window, high above, now not just a naked hole but a beautifully adorned sheet of stained glass, changed my perspective for me. These were the ruins of my life? Now they were whole and new, magnificent in every way.

As in a dream, I rose up on nothing and stood in the air before the round window and beheld the glowing, colorful image portrayed in it. A flying woman trailing a streak of blue light held a sword in both hands. She was dressed in pure white and darkness fled from her far below, at the bottom of the circle. The sword she carried was adorned with a great shimmering diamond at the hilt.

The sword was unique, but it wasn't quite the Sword of Light. I knew that Sword well—it didn't have a massive diamond studding the hilt like this one did.

Still, though, I knew who the woman was.

It was me.

CHAPTER X

Sawtooth Mountains of Idaho, Present Day

"YOU CANNOT CRUSH IT, break it, or trick it into going away," Kreios said. "The Bloodstone is not of this world, Michael—it must be sent back if it is to be overcome." Kreios paced in front of the fire, unsure if the boy had what it took to go on, to withstand the Bloodstone.

"What do you suggest?" Michael was tired, frustrated, and it showed on his face. They'd been at it for hours and come up with no better plan than to have Michael surreptitiously take the oath of the Seer and destroy the Brotherhood from within. But that was fraught with problems, one being that Michael had to live as the Seer and somehow keep himself from being overtaken by the most powerful form of evil in creation.

"What if we . . ." Kreios spoke aloud. It was a passing thought, but it might work.

"What if what? Kreios, what are you thinking?"

Kreios rushed into his study and rummaged through his books and scrolls. "Where are you hiding?" he muttered under his breath. Finding the right one, he returned to Michael.

"Are you going to share or keep all the good stuff to yourself?" Michael seemed to be in better spirits, and Kreios was glad for the distraction.

"This is a book covering the history of death, the grave, and Hades. It talks of the afterlife of the foulest, of the undead."

"And how does that help us? Are you planning on going there?"

Kreios held up a finger and paused, thinking. "You may be on to something, and if I am right, I think I found a way to get rid of the Bloodstone for good." Kreios permitted himself a modest half grin, but it disappeared when the earth began to tremble. Like a firebeast of ancient times about to break forth beneath the mountains, he could feel the thin place on which his house had been built beginning to change.

Michael sat up. "What's wrong? You have a funny look on your face."

"Do you not feel the earth groan?"

Michael knit his brows together. "No. I don't feel the earth groaning. What's going on?"

"I am not sure." Kreios went to the bookshelf on the far wall, slid a wooden panel aside, and turned on the display that was hidden there.

Michael whistled. "I see you did keep the cool stuff to yourself."

CNN flashed a banner across the bottom of the screen, and the announcer—a woman with a perfect complexion and long, dark hair—read her notes with a practiced voice.

"An earthquake surpassing a magnitude of twenty on the Richter scale that has occurred in the Pacific Ocean is predicted to set off a series of events such as we have never before seen in the recorded history of mankind. The series of tsunamis over the next few days may, in fact, be global. The president has declared a state of emergency. Everyone in the flood zones is encouraged to stay calm. We urge you not to panic."

The broadcast cut to a map of the world with large areas in red marked as the flood zones. Michael swore.

Kreios muttered a prayer to El. Many millions would die. "We are running out of time."

CHAPTER XI

Arabia, 788 B.C.

KREIOS WAS FORCED TO look on from a distance as his brother Zedkiel was beheaded by a tusked demon in the darkest shadows. He descended vengeance at the leading edge of his mind. The shadow of a figure took up his kinsman's sword and stole away.

Kreios touched down near Zedkiel's body. The tusked monster snorted at him, obviously unsure what to do next. Kreios made up its mind for it. He roared in anger at the tusked vermin, daring it to come try him. It ran off, searching for easier prey.

Kreios breathed, eyes wide as he knelt at Zedkiel's place of mortality.

He was gone.

The angel wept looking around for someone to kill.

QUIEL ARRIVED AT KE'ELEI via the horseshoe-shaped mountaintops that overlooked it. The battle below was a pitiful sight. What angelic forces had managed to muster themselves was no match for the legions of the Brotherhood arrayed against them. Those who belonged to El badly needed an equalizing force, something to give them half a chance.

Qiel thought about the liar Anael.

Qiel sought recompense more than anything else. He held out hope that his mother was not dead. It wasn't a simple revenge that he wanted most. It was more complicated than that because while he hated Anael for taking her from him, he reserved some of that hatred for Uriel herself. She had not kept him from the worst evil he had ever known, and yet she had kept him from any usable warning about it. Why did you allow this to happen to me, Mother? Why? He had never felt so unsupported and isolated.

But these thoughts dissipated quickly, and then he beheld the storm of red lightning in the valley below. His eyes told a corner's worth of the story, and instinct illuminated for him the rest of the page.

That is Anael. His hour has come.

Qiel knew how dangerous it was to allow these thoughts to inch past the gates of his mind, but his heart couldn't bear the torture any longer. He, therefore, released his thoughts into fury, unlocking those gates, throwing them open wide. He roared stirring his gift into thunder and flood.

Now would come monsters.

And real terror.

Elsewhere

MY DREAMS CONTINUED AS I moved in the far corners of my consciousness—or whatever it was I was doing. I walked along the seashore. I could see an expanse of colorful sands, the surf pounding along the boundary on one side, lush forests rising upward on the other.

"She?"

"Airel."

I had so many questions. I blurted them all out in my mind by the thousands in an instant. "Was that place—the ruins?"

"They are just a glimpse of your life."

I wondered what that was supposed to mean. "My life?" I asked, but there was only silence as I walked along the shore. My life was over, as far as I knew. But how did it get rebuilt? And what does it mean?

"These are but symbols for now, Airel. Do not stumble over their meanings. The real question is, do you know why you're here?"

"I don't even know where here is," I said.

"You've always known, girl." She sounded a bit like my father, a bit like Kreios. "You don't need me to tell you you're different."

Yeah, I thought. It's my curse.

"You did well enough."

"How?" I asked. "I was a total screwup. I never did anything with my life. I never became anyone important. I was always just putting out fires, reacting to the latest crisis or injury." I looked down and stopped. "I never did anything with my life."

"You did do something magnificent, though."

I began to cry. "What are you talking about? I lived a train of disasters. I fell hard for the worst boyfriend in history, the ultimate bad boy." I didn't want to admit that even now, I still loved Michael. "And it's because of me that Kim died." I stopped talking then.

"You're funny."

"How?"

"Because despite how vehemently you rail against people who judge you by what they see, you're doing the exact same thing to yourself."

I was silent.

"I can see your heart, though, Airel. And I see greatness. I saw how you were able to forgive Michael sincerely, even as the piercing fire of his betrayal still scalded your heart. And you continued to love him afterward, even though he was the source of so much pain. I saw how you loved Kim despite her behavior at the end of her life. You loved unconditionally, Airel. These are the things that matter."

"Why?"

"You did what matters," She said. "And what you did— matters."

I thought of Kim, Michael, my parents . . . and felt that not much of my life really mattered. But maybe that was what this dream was about—a way to process how I felt about who I was. Maybe this was my life flashing before my eyes.

CHAPTER XII

Glasgow, Scotland, Present Day

VALAC WORE FADED JEANS and an untucked white button-up shirt. He rode silently in the elevator, and when the doors opened, a beautiful woman in heels and a short skirt met him. Short enough to say things about her.

"Mr. Weston is expecting you. Follow me, please."

"My pleasure," Valac said as he licked his lips. He was a sensual being, and his time with Airel had awakened some of his buried desires.

Two tall solid wood doors opened as they approached. The woman stepped aside and he smiled as he looked her up and down. "My dear, won't you be joining us?"

"No," she said with a wicked smile.

"My heart breaks at this," Valac said, taking her hand and caressing it, looking her over once more as if he were shopping for snacks. "Maybe you can put me back together later tonight, at my hotel?" He did not wait for her answer. He stepped directly into a huge office yawning open before him. It took half the floor. The doors closed behind him before his host said a word.

"Valac. You come with good news, I hope." Jordan was standing beside his desk dressed impeccably, as usual. It's nice to see another man with taste.

"Airel is out of the picture." Valac smiled.

Jordan pursed his lips and nodded as he sipped water—or vodka—from a crystal glass. "I believe you have your reward, then. You did take her abilities?" Jordan pulled out his chair and sat behind his desk, smoking a small cigar.

"It does not work like that, Jiki. And we had a deal," Valac said, walking to the bank of windows and looking out at Glasgow through the beads of rain on the glass. "You wouldn't be foolish enough to think of betraying me, would you?"

"You completed half your mission. Her father yet lives."

Valac made a fist and ground his teeth together. "You change the terms once again, a fact I'm going to allow one last time." Valac turned to face him. "I tell you, if you ever send another team in front of me—"

"I had to be sure. Calm yourself. Airel is a powerful half-breed, and it pays to be careful in this line of work."

"It was a mistake not to trust me."

Jordan snorted. "I trust no one." He stood putting down his cigar and blowing a ring of smoke. "The Alexander is fighting his true calling, and my sources have found a link to the Other."

Valac had heard the rumors of the Other, the one who was in line to be Seer before the Alexander. He didn't really care, but it was interesting that Airel's father would be somehow involved. "What does he have to do with the Other?"

"He may know his identity—it could be lost somewhere in his mind. Blood never lies, Valac."

Valac grew tired of this conversation. "As much as I would love to talk of the Seer, blood, and even who might win the Super Bowl," he said, looking toward the doors, "I have a date with Miss Legs-for-days out there tonight and I need a nap first. If you don't mind, I'll be on my way."

Jordan smiled. "I will pay you, of course. And I have a new job you may be interested in." He held up a slip of paper and Valac took it. "I will double your price, but he must go willingly."

Valac read the note and nodded. "Payment first. What you owe me plus the full amount, up front, for this one."

Jordan shrugged. "Agreed."

"Now, tell me your secretary is single."

"Does it matter?"

Valac smirked. "No, I guess not."

"Just don't eat her."

"You take the fun out of everything."

"I enjoy her too," Jordan said, "but in different ways. I want to keep her around a while longer."

Valac sighed. "Will you allow me at least a finger? Maybe two?"

Elsewhere

I BECAME AWARE OF the room my body was in. There came to my ears the sound of machines pumping. I felt tubes running down my throat and saw my mom withering away next to me. She was there, but her eyes were empty and void.

Michael didn't come back. Is he gone forever? Where's Ellie—where's Kim? Then I remembered her funeral, the rain, and my tears.

My heart was awake for the first time since my return to Boise.

I had been pushing everyone in my life away. Maybe my dreams
were the lifeline, the reason I lay here in a coma. I was supposed
to realize something crucial. I didn't feel complete. There was still
something I was supposed to see—learn.

Like most dreams, when I woke I had a hard time remembering
exactly what had happened. It was more feeling than memory. There
was a small stone house, a book—but not my Book. It was The
Book. She talked to me as if she were a real person, standing beside
me in the form of a little girl.

I saw my story overlaid with hers. "I am in every part of your
life, Airel. I love you, and your mistakes and triumphs are mine
too."

I still didn't understand what it all meant. What am I supposed
to see?

I saw the earth made of ink, the people of paper. All were born
and plunged into the blackness, but not all had to remain living in
the darkness.

I felt as if I'd been walking the earth as a ghost ever since
Stanley had plunged his sword into my heart. I was out of order; my
life was artificial.

But how . . .?

"Your Book, as is the same with all the Books, was never
intended to be used as anything other than to tell the unflinching
story of your life, warts and all. That is why it is so dangerous, so
powerful. But when Michael wrote in it, he changed the proper
order."

I thought about this. You mean that when he wrote in my Book,
he overruled the story in The Book?

"Michael's actions changed everything, Airel."

You mean nothing I lived was real?

"Tell me, if reality is an illusion, how real can it be? Michael took something from you that you hadn't offered to him. And yet you did not resist. Not even then."

I wanted to weep. Was none of it real?

"Oh, it was very real. That is why the consequences will be so heavy."

This is why I'm here. This was why everything was falling apart. I was supposed to die that day. Drown. What Michael had done, he did in his grief, out of love, but he set things in motion no one could have predicted.

What do I do?

"Forgive."

I don't understand.

"Forgive him, forgive yourself; stop letting the past rule over you. This is why you are here, Airel. To let go of the things that hold you back so when the time comes, you can do what you were born to do."

CHAPTER XIII

Amsterdam, Present Day

JOHN CROSS MANAGED TO bribe his way onto an international flight to Europe. That had been too expensive, leaving him cash poor and not sure how he was going to get to Dubai. He sat in the terminal at Schiphol in Amsterdam, nursing a migraine from the cigarette smoke, and frustrated to be in this position. Dubai was one of the last fully functional urban centers in the world, and the only contact he still trusted lived in Dubai.

He'd had enough time to make a decision. The attack at his house had happened a week ago now, and he wouldn't sit by helplessly to await his daughter's death. His wife was lost to him, grief overtaking her—and some guilt, to be sure–so it was either sit around or find some answers. He was not good at sitting around.

There weren't that many people milling about. Schiphol was traditionally a very busy place, but today—and probably lately, John mused—it was a shell of itself. The only people travelling these days were those with means or connections or both. Weirdly, all of them seemed to be smokers. I'll never really get Europeans. The more things change . . .

Meanwhile, the world had changed, and, it seemed to John, irrevocably. Nearly a billion people—these were the best estimates—had perished in the Great Pacific Quake and the Global Tsunami, which, coincidentally, had happened on the exact same day the dragon dinosaur demon showed up in his daughter's bedroom.

Oh, what fun we had.

John suffered a twitching shiver at the memory of it. The big one had a head, sure. But its face was in its abdomen. That's why all those head shots were so ineffective, but the body shots had taken it out. What chilled him most was that the beast's face was human. Well . . . vaguely. The smaller one had vanished except for a pile of ash in the living room. John wondered if the thing was dead or on the run.

When he had calmed himself enough to examine the reason of the home invasion—because there was always a purpose behind violence of any sort—he didn't have to search Airel's room very long until he'd found it. A little black book, under the mattress— right where he'd hidden his own most valuable treasures as a youth. It was volume III of The Book of the Brotherhood, and when he first read those words, the claws of fear raked across his heart, tracing veins of ice deep and fast.

These assailants had been one military unit—albeit demonic, which he wasn't sure he could believe even now. Had they had come to retrieve this book? Why Airel had possession of it in the first place really puzzled him, though. What had she gotten herself mixed up in? The Alexander boy had something to do with it, surely.

But of course he opened it. Who wouldn't? Huddled in a corner of his daughter's bedroom, pulse pounding like a scared little boy, the corpse of a demon in the hallway, he had read. In five minutes,

the necessary connections fired across his synapses and he knew
that PILLBOX had set him up on a suicide mission in Glasgow to
retrieve the most powerful talisman under the sun—the Bloodstone.

John didn't fully understand it all, and upon reading the book,
he'd found opening up before him yet another set of problems he
had to address. They had tried to kill him twice now. Airel was
involved too, evidently. They should have kept her out of it—or
at least kept him out of it. Either way, he could taste blood. Self-
defense was altogether a different flavor than fatherly rage, though.

After having had a week to mull things over and do a little of
his own research, John decided that Dubai was the place to start. He
would meet his contact—he did not inform him of the visit; some
things were better to do without announcement—and then retrace
his steps to find out where the Bloodstone went and who was trying
to kill him. Airel was in a coma because of all this. Someone is
going to pay.

He glanced at his carryon. The book was tucked away in there
safely. No need to get it out right now and read it; he had already
read it ten times at least. The dirty compulsion was strong, though. I
need a cigarette myself, come to think of it. John looked around the
lounge. There was a man seated across from him who was smoking.
He had an expensive look to him. "Hey, buddy. Bum a smoke from
ya?"

The man looked up. Annoyance flashed across his features, but
he reached into his suit coat pocket and fished out a blue pack of
Gauloises anyway. "Oui. Vous voilà."

John stood and walked to him, taking the proffered cigarette
from the Frenchman's casual hand. "Merci." He stooped as the
Frenchman lit it for him. He stood, took a long drag, and nearly
choked. That's really strong.

The Frenchman smirked acidly at him and shrugged. "Liberté

tojours." His shoulders bounced once or twice in light mirth.

John turned back toward his seat, giving him a limp salute. "Vive la France, buddy."

The Frenchman gave a not-impolite little snort. "Americain, yes?"

John sat. "Isn't it obvious?"

"What brings you to the continent?" he asked, his English actually quite good. "Business?"

John thought about it before answering. "You could say I'm seeing the sights. I'm on my way elsewhere."

The Frenchman took a drag and then exhaled. "Ah." The hand with the cigarette traced an arc in the air before it came to rest at his side.

What is it with the French? They do everything with artistic flair.

"Than it is business."

"You're reading me like a book. Well . . . you might as well know the title. Name's Jim." Hey, close enough. Maybe he'll buy it.

"Pierre-Henri." Pierre stood and then reached to shake John's hand. "Pleasure. May I?"

John moved his carryon aside. "Oui. By all means, please." He took another drag and felt nauseated. Perhaps this is the price of a friend. "And you? What brings you to Amsterdam, Pierre?"

Pierre looked at him with a flash of caution. "It is business, mon ami."

"Good." John nodded, "So we're both just a couple of bull salesmen."

Pierre laughed.

Yes, John thought, friend-making strategy 101. He could usually get a laugh out of someone. Perhaps he could get more out of "Monsieur Moreau" or whoever he was. "So you headed home now?"

"Oh no, no," Pierre said. His face became darker now. "No, frère Jim, I can never go back there. France is on fire, as I am sure you know." He took a drag. "I flee to safer climes."

"I'm sorry for your loss," John said. "So is it Dubai, then? Or Stockholm?"

"Dubai, Jim—you are very smart. Not everyone knows this. It is one or the other now, is it not? And I am afraid my Swedish is not so good." Pierre smiled, and it was tragic.

John was struck in that moment. His conscience was unusually wide awake. "Pierre, I gotta shoot straight because I feel like I can trust you. There's something in your eyes that tells me you're a quality person. I'm just not sure who I can trust these days, so I lied to you about who I am." John extended his hand once more. "John Cross."

"Ah," Pierre said, shaking his hand. "I see." His face registered that gears were meshing behind the scenes and that he was thinking things over. "Your business in Dubai—it is very serious, is it not?"

"Yes, Pierre. It is very serious." John considered things for a moment. "Thanks again for the cigarette."

"You like?"

"No, it was horrible."

Pierre belly laughed at this. "This is true; they are terrible. I've been meaning to give them up for years now." He stubbed out his cigarette in the adjacent ashtray. "Today is the day."

John stood. "Buy you a drink to celebrate?"

Pierre stood as well. "Oui, monsieur. We shall trade one vice for another. You will pay dearly, though, I must warn you. I do not take lightly this offense of you talking bad about my Gauloises. These are a French institution, very nationalistic."

"Two drinks, then. At least." John clapped him on the back as he grabbed his luggage and they walked. The tiniest part of him, that which was still unsullied and uncynical, had truly made a friend in Pierre, truly liked him. The other ninety-nine percent, though, was busy calculating how and when to make the most use of this new potential asset.

JOHN AND PIERRE SAT and talked over vodka martinis at first, switching to club soda—over here they called it "sparkling water"—pretty quickly. John told Pierre he was searching for information about a collection of rare books. He told a story about his own recent personal tragedies involving his daughter, but most of it was a lie. He wasn't going to trust anyone anymore. He knew better—this was business.

He let Pierre talk, gave him enough information to keep him talking, and then found that Pierre's situation was similar to his own. He had lost his two sons, about college age, in the riots that had swept France in months prior. His boys had joined a revolutionary militia and been killed in action near his home just outside of Lyon. His wife hanged herself in the closet days later. She had seen too much, and Pierre was, like John, a man with little to lose anymore, save his life.

Pierre was a man with resources, and it wasn't long until John realized that his new friend was his ticket to Dubai.

"I want you to meet someone when we get to Dubai, John. He's a man of means. I believe he can help you. I'll even flip for the airline tickets."

John set his glass on the table and leaned back in his chair. "Helping me with my obsession? No, I won't have it. I hate to be a tagalong, and you paying for my ticket is too much."

Pierre waved his hand in the air dismissively. "Nonsense. Times are hard, with the earthquake and so many millions of people dying. The world is on fire, John. We need to band together, to help a friend. Besides, I'm good at reading people, and you, John Cross, are a good man."

Hook, line, and sinker. "Thanks, Pierre. This means more than you'll ever know. And like I said, as soon as we get in, I'll pay you back. The man I'm seeing owes me, and he'll make it right."

"It will be what it will be. Now, this man I want you to meet, he is someone who knows things, knows of this book you speak of, I am sure of it. I really think he can direct you to the right people at the very least. It's all about who you know, John."

John lifted his glass. "I'll drink to that."

CHAPTER XIV

Arabia, 788 B.C.

PIANKHY DID NOT BELIEVE the first few reports as they came to him, but eventually he had to turn aside from the command of his forces and investigate. "Sea monsters in the forest; it is absurd." He was more than a little angered by these rumors because in the end, it was just another distraction from the battle, from inevitable martial glory.

But he could not ignore them. Too many trusted lieutenants had reported these things. The looks on their faces—stark fear—were most compelling.

He stalked over scorched earth to the rear, the areas where his legions had trampled on their way to the breached walls of Ke'elei. The battle had reached a turning point; all that lay ahead was the mop-up, the final kills. And now he had to divert his all-too-valuable attention to look into children's tales.

"There, my general," a lieutenant said. "It writhes."

Piankhy looked below them to a clearing where his officer pointed. Indeed, there it was, tentacles slashing out in a large radius, its head as big as three chariots side by side—a beast from the depths of the sea, sickly pink, glistening, terrible. Beneath the monster sprung up foamy fountains of seawater, lifting his men from their feet, drowning horses, and tilting the battle in favor of the sea gods. Piankhy now felt for the first time in his life the tangible seizure of terror. It was a stricture about his throat. His eyes began to water as he said, "Are there more?"

The lieutenant replied, "Yes, my general. Many."

URIEL COULD NOT KNOW it as she involuntarily spread every molecule of her power throughout the substrata, but there would be unintended consequences for what was happening. She did not know what had manifested in her son, Qiel, how potent his gift was—especially when motivated by fear and revenge.

She did not know, for instance, that her son had drawn near, that he was close to losing control. But even if she had known it, there was nothing she could have done to prevent what happened; she was a puppet on a string. This she would nevertheless lament in the centuries to come and blame herself above all others—if Ke'elei were to fall, the powers of darkness would need to conjure up the perfect storm. She helped to provide it.

She wouldn't have called it liquefaction as scientists in the 20th century would do, but in this case, a name for the phenomenon was irrelevant, semantics. Combined with what Qiel was capable of doing, what he was indeed now doing above ground—calling the seas up from the depths of the earth, those immense gates El had opened in the Great Flood—Ke'elei's destruction was imminent.

In short, her power to dissemble was hijacked by the overwhelming power of the Bloodstone. When she had taken herself apart and blended with the Stone in her attempt to steal it, the damage was total and immediate. She became an automaton, a slave. And the stone held the bit, the bridle, and the whip.

The moment had arrived.

She had deployed herself in a radius of several leagues in the bedrock under the city. Now with a single thought, she triggered her power, and every particle of earth she touched came unglued. As gravity called the mass downward like sand in an hourglass, Qiel called the sea upward from below.

It would create a sinkhole leagues across, and it would devour every man, angel, and demon within reach of its jaws.

ABOVE GROUND, URIEL MOVED as a shadow. She could feel the ground begin to tremble underfoot. The Brotherhood's main force had breached the city wall in three places, not the least of which was the main gate. The barbican was now engulfed in flames. Demons flew, dropped from the sky, and took the city from above. The angelic army was growing weak and would soon be overcome.

Uriel heard the rushing of water but paid no mind. She had one task remaining, and than she knew the Bloodstone would cast her aside like so much trash. She had never felt so conflicted before. The last thing she had to do was the last thing she wanted to do.

Yamanu. Teacher of the shadowing arts. He stood not far off, leaning against an archway, breathing in ragged gulps, his back heaving with many sorrows. He was weeping. He no doubt wept for the fall of the City of Refuge, for the loss of so many of his kind, for Anael's heartless betrayal—one compounded, no doubt, into many over the centuries, given what she knew of him.

Uriel could feel Zedkiel's sword in her hand as she approached her uncle to take his life. She could feel a tear escape and roll down her smoke-smudged cheek as she understood what she was going to be forced to do.

QIEL DESCENDED FROM THE heights to the city, having opened the floodgates upon the Brotherhood. Ancient ones—creatures that would live on only in later man's fairy tales as dragons, dinosaurs, and monsters—now stalked the forests. The seas welled up from below and permeated the battlefield, destroying most of the enemy's main force and giving the monsters of the sea great advantage.

Qiel had learned and done much since that day in the tower, when he first discovered his affinity for water and its power. He discovered a kinship with sea beasts; he was able to control Leviathan with his mind. He could summon the floods from below and make the skies precipitate.

And he had learned he was desperate. While he harbored animosity for his mother because of her failure to protect him, both from outside forces as well as himself, he would do anything to find her and free her.

Desperate things.

Even things with little hope of success.

Like breaking the Brotherhood from the inside.

In the forest below, men drowned in a tidal wave he produced with his mind. Water twisted around him like the arms of an octopus as he grabbed demons out of the air and tore them in half. Others he slapped to the ground, sending daggers of frozen seawater deep into their flesh. His control over the element was incredible even to himself. Somehow the water knew what he wanted, and it responded with total obedience.

But one last foe remained to Qiel.

Anael.

He hovered over the city wreathed in red lightning, striking out at any, man or angel, who dared to venture through the streets. Qiel could feel the earth tremble beneath him, and it caused him to dread. If his mother was dead, he feared what he would do. Pray, Anael, for your sake that she lives.

There remained to him yet one more way to wage war against this enemy. Precipitation. As Qiel thought it, the rains began and heavy hailstones fell. At first, they were light and spitting, but it soon augmented into a monsoon, drenching and pelting everything in the valley. Anael raged on in the sky, striking out against the innocents below him with bursts of lightning one after another.

Qiel did not understand with his reason why in order to seal the victory he needed to force Anael to touch the earth, but he knew it nevertheless. He sensed by instinct that it was not enough that Anael was now soaked. Bring him to ground was all he could think, so he did.

From the middle of the sky directly over Anael's head, Qiel caused the rains to intensify, and under this waterfall Anael became completely submerged and began to fall. Qiel could feel how he was suffocating within it, and it made him smile.

The force of the waterfall's weight carried the traitor down and down, closer to the earth. Anael hovered a few handbreadths above the ground, the waterfall crashing over him. Then with a cracking peal of thunder, a thick red arc of lightning surged from the ground, through the gathering waters, and into Anael.

He fell, quiet and motionless.

Qiel allowed the waters to subside.

Pinning him down with daggers of ice, Qiel drew near. Anael's arms and feet were bleeding, turning the water puddled around him to red. The ice daggers stuck out of his flesh like huge nails. "You took my mother," Qiel said. "Where is she? Does she live?"

Anael coughed up blood and laughed. "She is your mother no more, my son. She now belongs to the Bloodstone."

Qiel did not understand what the old man was saying. "Shut your mouth. You turned me into this monster. You activated these powers. Now you shall reap your just reward." When Qiel raised his hands to strike, Anael lifted his hands and smiled, and Qiel hesitated, thinking. Mother only ever told me the smallest bits and pieces about what we both truly are. He was hungry to know the nature of the blood that now ran in his veins.

Anael gurgled. It was a laugh. "He hesitates. But why?"

Qiel growled. "Why does a young man seek a sage, old man?"

Anael sneered. "Answers. You hunger for an answer to the riddle of what you are. Oh, what's to become of me?" he mocked. "Come close, my son. I have the answers—I can tell you everything you want to know."

"What price? Your life, I suppose?"

Anael coughed up more blood and shook his head. "No, boy. I want yours."

Qiel could not mask his surprise.

Anael waved a hand, dismissing his fears. "A simple trade— your life for your mother's."

Qiel lowered his hand. It wasn't strictly in surrender, but the gesture also wasn't devoid of consideration. "Why?"

Anael writhed in pain. "I die, and you torture me with ridiculous questions. Time is short. Yes or no?"

"Who am I that you would want me over her?"

Anael gestured to the chaos around them, above and below them. "You are a perfect contradiction—a Son of El with the blood of the Brotherhood running through you. You are a half-breed able to wield the power of El and to resist the curse of the Brotherhood."

He moved his hands as if casting a spell. "Imagine."

Qiel had to admit that he had already done such things. And more.

"You are the next Seer, my son. The heir to the throne."

Qiel clenched his fists and stepped backward. "No."

Anael's eyes reddened as his features fell slack. "You will, boy. Or your mother will surely die."

KREIOS FOUND HIS OLD friend lying facedown in the rain. This was the last of the pureblood angels of El.

Save for one.

Kreios. And Kreios would be the last.

Yamanu was dead, struck down with Zedkiel's own sword. Kreios, El's Angel of Death, knelt over the warm corpse of his companion and lamented all. He was not given, but an instant to grieve. There was a mighty rumble as the ground gave way beneath everything he could see.

Kreios took slowly to the sky, hovering and staring in shock as Yamanu's body was taken down and consigned to this mass grave, his end, their end, the loss of everything Kreios and his kind had ever had together. It all crashed in upon itself and sank down into the ground, swallowed up by the earth.

Ke'elei was gone.

CHAPTER XV

Elsewhere

THERE WERE PEOPLE IN my room, talking excitedly. I searched for Mom. She was not in her usual chair by the window. I couldn't turn my head or move, so I was limited to what I could see from my back.

Someone said, "Keep administering CPR. Tell the nurse to get a defibrillator in here now." Silence. Then, "How long has she been like this?"

"I don't know. We check in on the patient once per shift," a woman said.

More commotion. Somebody said, "Clear," several times and there was a thumping sound. Two men came in with a stretcher and bent down. My mom was lifted into place on it and taken out in a big rush as I screamed for her in the silent hell of my own head. I caught a glimpse of her face—it was drawn, hollow, lifeless.

I was alone in the room. I cried and cried, but the tears never surfaced on my face. I cursed my father for not being here. Where is he?

She whispered again, drawing me into safer places where I

could find rest. I was tired, alone, and unable to control what was happening to me. "There remains before you your darkest hour, Airel. Your resolve and desire will face their greatest testing." I could feel in She's voice both sadness and solid reassurance that these things were precisely as they should be. "You will yet be brought to the pinnacle of your life. There you must make your last choice between darkness and light. You will need this."

As I looked, it was as if I was watching myself from above. There in front of me appeared the Sword of Light. I would know that blade anywhere.

"It is El's Sword. He offers it freely to you for another season. Airel," She said. "Wake up—awaken!"

I did, but I was no longer in the hospital bed. I was somewhere else, somewhere beautiful. I saw a door hovering before me without handle or frame. I knew this door . . . long ago I'd seen it in my dreams, in my imagination, as I'd read the Book of Kreios.

I held the Sword of Light aloft for the first time in forever. A shout rang out and resonated within the molecules of the blade, which I noticed was different now. At the bisection of the blade and the guard, right at the hilt, there was a perfect circle cutting through, admitting light, air.

I swung it around a few times. It seemed to make the blade faster. Guadagnare. Stocatta.

I walked toward the door, sword in hand, and it opened. My eyes locked onto the burning black globe I beheld through the doorway. A world on fire.

I was going home. I was going back to where it had all started, and I would put an end to what was not meant to be.

Moments later, pain knifed through me. I could feel the extent of my body, the limits of my frame, and it was awkward and weird. My lungs burned—air was being forced down into me through tubes. My eyes opened and I screamed for help.

Independence, Missouri, Present Day

ELLIE HAD A THEORY she hoped would buy her a little more time. She was already very weak, so it was a last ditch effort even to try it.

As she dissolved from the couch in her father's library and scattered to the winds, she isolated the contagion of the Mark in her body, placing it away from her, in quarantine. She knew it was temporary at best, since—and she could feel this—the source it fed upon was her heart, but maybe she could buy a couple of weeks. The Mark's infection was beyond her powers to overcome. She would do what she could to delay the inevitable as long as possible. Just like any driven human determined to save the world.

She didn't know what would happen. When she gathered herself back together under a tree in the parking lot of the Midwest Genealogy Center in Independence, Missouri, she had readied herself for anything.

She'd thought it might kill her. But in fact, she felt better than she had in a long time, and she kicked herself for not trying it sooner. *I feel like a new woman. Like I've just had the best spa day ever.*

She walked inside.

The receptionist looked up at her. "Welcome to the largest facility for genealogies in the world. How may I help y—oh, wow. Can I just say . . . I just love your hair."

"Why, thanks," Ellie said. "I'm kinda partial myself." She gave a mild curtsy.

The receptionist, a round, dowdy-looking woman dressed in the full range of browns, giggled. "We don't get many people around here sporting that look."

"Well, I've stuck with what works. In and out of season." For thousands of years. "So, ah. . ." Ellie looked around for a nameplate. "So, Brenda. Where are the C's? I've got some research to do."

"Oh, of course." Brenda peeled her eyes from Ellie's electric blue mane and shoved a clipboard forward. "Sign in, and then you'll want to take the elevator to level two. You're so dang cute." Brenda giggled again.

Ellie smiled and registered and went to the second floor. After talking to three different people, she was ushered to a small room with no windows and a computer sitting on a simple desk.

As she looked through the boxes of documents that traced the Cross family tree upward from Airel to John, the trail ended. John Cross apparently had no parents, no family. No past. Which meant, "Extremely complicated." Ellie grasped at her pounding chest and coughed. Maybe not two weeks. Maybe two days.

She needed to get moving then.

Airel mentioned grandparents—they must have been on her mom's side.

She thought back to her son. She always wondered what became of him. He must have had children—otherwise, Airel would never have been born. Without angelic blood, the family line would not have been able to continue. But Qiel was lost and assumed dead ages ago. After Ke'elei, she herself had gone off the grid. She'd thought about it a lot, but never so much as she had in the last few weeks.

Wait a minute. What if I'm looking at the wrong parent?

What if it was Airel's mother who carried the bloodline? What do I even know of my own family tree?

Ellie cursed. She had to start over.

She shoved the box aside and moved to the computer. There had to be something here, anything that could give her answers as to who Airel's family were. It had started out as a hunch, an itch that needed to be scratched, but her intuition about John Cross was turning out to be a dead end.

No matter. Maybe Maggie Cross would turn up something.

She didn't even know what she was really after. Maybe she needed to feel connected to her own past by finding out about Airel's. Or maybe the thought of dying—of the Mark taking her once and for all—made her want to see what she'd missed.

All those years in hiding, running from this . . . and now that it's the only thing I want, it's the only thing I can't have.

Ellie sat back, letting the computer do its search again and again. After an hour of digging, she had come up with nothing. Maggie Cross was much easier to trace. Maggie had a past, she had a documented history. Once Ellie had found her maiden name, she was able to rule her out. Her ancestry was clear. Airel's mother was purebred human. And that meant only one thing.

It was down to John Cross again.

What are you hiding, John?

PART TWELVE

THE UNMAKING

CHAPTER I

Arabia, 788 B.C.

QIEL WATCHED AS THE city of Ke'elei sank forever down, swallowed whole by the hungry earth. He didn't believe in Sheol, but he was beginning to reconsider as his eyes saw things which they protested, stubbornly, were not real. Wave upon wave clapped together, capping in peaks of white foam rendered pink by blood and sucking down into the crater, drowning most of the Brotherhood army along with every inhabitant of the city.

The sea was no respecter of allegiances. All flesh tasted the bitterness of death in its swirling, icy grip.

Lying in Piankhy's tent, Anael lived on, laboring to breathe, the general of the Brotherhood armies stooped low over his face, straining to hear his last words. Piankhy spoke in a hush with Anael, whispers Qiel could not hear as he looked on from the other side of the general's tent. His mind raced searching for ways to escape his doom—it was his mother's life or his. All of his considerable powers were impotent now. How could he save his mother if he didn't know the first thing about how to find her? The best he could do was hold on and see where this game would spit him out.

Piankhy stood. "Anael is dead," he said as if the news should have made someone sorry.

"Good," Qiel said. "May he burn in hell for a thousand eternities." Qiel spat and watched as it soaked into the Persian rug on which they stood. "It's the least he deserves."

"And what of you, Qiel? What is it you deserve?"

Qiel didn't want to say. "Tell me what he told you."

The general walked to a nearby table and took up a pomegranate, polishing it against his sash. "Surely you don't really want to know."

"What deal did you broker with the old wretch? Tell me. I want just one thing now. I can certainly sweeten the deal for you."

Piankhy laughed. "Really? That is indeed surprising. I did not know you had . . . shall we say . . . eternal authority."

Qiel paused. *The old traitor must have more power than I imagined.* Thoughts crashed together in his head like waves, and in the wake of it he wondered if Anael lived on, if he had somehow become Seer forever, if he had, like a seed, gone dormant, awaiting the most opportune time. *What if he is inside the Stone?* Qiel could taste malevolence in the tent, hovering near.

"What say you?" The general turned loose of the pomegranate and slipped a hand beneath his sash. "Would you like to be the next recipient of this?" He withdrew his hand, producing a heavy iron chain, and from the end of it swung a stone so red it was almost black.

Qiel found himself holding his breath. He watched as the stone began to glow, as it began to swing like a pendulum ever closer to him, moving at last in defiance of all gravity, hovering at the limit of its leash, the chain stretched taut and horizontal from the hand of the Brotherhood general across the tent, the stone straining at its bonds, trying to get to Qiel.

"Mmm. It wants you, but do you want it?"

Qiel considered. "My mother—she lives?"

Piankhy shrugged. "I suppose so."

"Deliver her to me. Then I will take up the Bloodstone. I will be your Seer."

"Anael was crafty," he said, teasing the chain now only by finger and thumb. The stone hummed louder, pulsing, its red rich and decadent. "That was what he proposed to me, I must admit."

Qiel doubted this, but as the stone grew louder in his ears, his doubts began to fade.

"I could not have planned a better solution to our problem. I am gladdened that you came to a reasonable conclusion so fast."

The Brotherhood was lost without a Seer, a leader to steer the horde into all unrighteousness and every dark strategy of the just rebellion. And the line of Kreios, most powerful of all the Fallen, lay fallow and broken, disused, until Qiel was born. And activated.

Qiel's virtues were self-evident—he was human, he was angelic . . . and he would be, as soon as he agreed and fulfilled the terms of the contract, demonic. He could be the most powerful being on earth. "Only let Uriel go free. Then you may have me."

Piankhy nodded. He chanted an incantation in a dark tongue, words Qiel imagined Anael might have used. A cloud of vapor formed in front of Qiel's eyes and became a shadow, and in this shadow, he could see his mother's face. She was seized with terror. As fast as it had appeared, it was taken away, her essence blown to the farthest reaches of the earth.

The general laughed. "She is free. She is broken, but she is free. Now fulfill your duty and say the words that will seal the transaction, boy, the words that even now are burning in your mind."

Qiel fell into a trance and found his lips forming these words: "I pledge life and soul to the Brotherhood. This life is not mine; there is only the Brotherhood, the clean nothingness. I swear in blood I shall soldier for my Brothers. Brothers in blood, brothers in death, brothers in the fires of Hell. And I their Seer." The stone was close now and Qiel touched it, sealing the deal.

His world became red.

Piankhy wound the iron chain around Qiel's neck and bowed low, his face touching the ground. "My brother. My Seer."

URIEL THOUGHT SHE HAD died when the Bloodstone released her. All at once she converged into one place again, within the heavy black fabric walls of the tent. She saw a glimpse of her son, a sight that broke her heart, for she could see what was in his eyes. But it was over too soon and she was in the wind again, taken leagues away from him. With what little strength remained to her, she reassembled and collapsed on the face of the mountainside, gasping for air.

She breathed her first breath and squinted her eyes, feeling the pain of both.

Water was soaking her cloak. She scrambled to her feet, a mad craving rooted deep within her heart, an addiction of blackest passion for the stone. All she wanted was more, to be rejoined to the Bloodstone, to feel cocooned within its terrible facets again, and safe inside the nothingness of it. Red and beautiful, it was evil, wonderful.

But then she looked to the horizon. Over a small rise, she saw it and cried out. This is all that is left of the beloved city. The valley that was once bedecked in hopeful tones of green, open and bright and full that led up to the city, was now a slough of mud and the putrid stench of the sea, the dying, and the dead. The mountain, once white, was now nothing but a black hole. Water poured into it. As she looked on in disbelief, the water began to calm and diminish. The mountain, now sheared clean of the evidence, stood over a dark lake. The troubled surface spread itself in the well of the hole, a vast silent witness covering the affronts just under its muddy flood.

The torrent had taken the city and killed most of the Brotherhood army and anyone else unable to fly to escape.

Uriel was a part of that. She had killed her own family, had betrayed her own. Now she was left with nothing. The Bloodstone had confiscated everything and spit her out when she ceased to be useful.

In the dread space of this waste, her thoughts turned reflexively to her only son, Qiel. He was the only, the last person she loved. The last person she thought she could ever love. *What has happened to you, son?*

"Qiel. Where are you?" She flew over the lake, searching for survivors. She hoped and prayed to El that her son yet lived. Nothing remained—the last of the Brotherhood horde had fled. A lone tent stood on a lump in the morass of what was left in the valley.

She flew there because there was nowhere else.

Empty. All gone. Only lying on a cot in the tent was the shriveled body of Anael, already in decay. Her longstanding adversary, the only one who knew where her son might be—if he was still alive—and he lay here dead.

Uriel cursed the heavens and fell to her knees and wept. Her heart broke under the weight of her guilt. Qiel was lost. Her father was gone. Her family and friends were buried under a murderous sea. *And it is my fault.* She was a traitor, she was the one who had abandoned all, she was the one who had raised her fist to El.

This was her reward.

Wiping her face, Uriel stood. She had to find her son. She had to know whether he was alive or dead. One man would know. Yshmial. The boy's father.

CHAPTER II

Sawtooth Mountains of Idaho, Present Day

IT WAS A CIRCUS at the hospital when I came to. I was pulling tubes and wires from my body as I jumped from the bed. My first thought, when I recognized the room, was Mom.

"Where is my mom?"

A nurse came in, a big dude with dark skin dressed in powder-blue scrubs. "Whoa, little lady. You need to sit back down here." He was the first one to see me post coma, and his eyes betrayed more than a little surprise.

"Where is my mom?"

The nurse put his hands on my shoulders and tried to force me back toward the bed. "Sit, little lady."

I wasn't thinking. I shrugged his hands off me, kneed him in the solar plexus, and when he doubled over, I turned him around and put him in an arm bar hold. "Where. Is. My. Mom?" I whispered into his ear.

"Ow," he said. "Hold on, little lady. Just let me go. You musta been having one trippy nightmare. Justin ain't gon' hurt you. Just let me go."

So I did.

Then there were doctors and specialists, pouring in and swarming me like demons. One wanted to check my vitals. Another had a stethoscope. Still another was trying to get me to lie back down on the bed. All of them were using the language of health professionals, full of jargon and professional interest.

I'd had enough of this crap. "Listen up," I said, giving all of them a violent shove and transitioning into a low hover, only half a foot above the floor, the blue light of my wake glowing beneath my feet. "One of you is going to tell me where my mom is." I noticed I was wearing only a hospital gown. "And then I'm going to get my clothes on and get out of here. Understood?"

Stark fear. They all scrambled to their feet and ran out of the room, except one. Big Justin, in the powder-blue scrubs.

Fear was there in his big brown eyes, but it was mixed with so much compassion, I knew what he was about to say next. "Yo momma's dead, little lady. She is dead. I'm so sorry."

I came back to earth.

"And my dad? Michael? Ellie?"

"Nobody's here for you, miss. I'm so sorry." He looked down. "Please don't hurt me."

"I won't hurt you. I'm sorry if I did."

I found my clothes and gathered them up. "Hey, Justin, do you mind, uh, standing guard for me?" I motioned to the door.

He blushed, which, for a black man as dark as he was, astounded me. I smiled my first smile at that. He beat feet, the door slamming behind him, and I got dressed as fast as I could.

I looked out the window and saw that my room was up on the eighth floor. I opened it wide. "This would have been a problem not too long ago," I said, spying the stunned look on Justin's face through the opening door over my shoulder. "But it's simple now." I stepped out into nothing. "And it's the only way."

I headed for the only place I knew was safe anymore.

The house of Kreios.

I reached out with my mind and called for Ellie, for Kreios.

Nothing.

I flew like a rocket, my blue contrail of light behind me, a blur in the sulfuric night skies, confused and scared. I'd never felt so alone and yet never felt so sure—sure of who I was and what I was supposed to do now.

My mom was dead. My sweet, innocent mother, the woman who raised me, the sensitive eccentric of the family, the lady whose chair in the living room was always reserved for her alone, the woman who dug in the dirt of the garden and made everything grow bright and beautiful. She was gone forever now. And I didn't know what to do about it, much less what to think or how to feel.

All I could think of was my grandfather and my need to find him. My grandfather. The Angel of Death.

As I blazed through the sky, I saw the radiance of light that now emanated from within me, lighting up my surroundings. The Sword of Light came to my hand. My vision was very clear and it gave me groundspeed, altitude, and other data, just like always. As I looked back over my shoulder, I could see that the halo of dazzling light that emanated from my body now took the form of wings. These blurred from pure white into cool hot blue, demarcating my path in the heavens.

Warning bells in my head. I remembered the "pact" my forebears had been forced to make with the Brotherhood, promising not to fly. I figured the Brotherhood would find me to be especially offensive right now. You know what? I don't give a rip. Come and get me. See how much you regret it. My emotions were finding their center in anger right now, and I knew that made me very dangerous.

Before I realized the fabric of the world had been drawn so thin, the only way I could get to the house of Kreios was to use the door in the forest floor. But now I could see the skies and the waterfall clearly, and the back patio, the long staircase leading to the meadow below. I passed through the limitations of time, physical space, and memory, touching down at the back door.

It was daylight here. The snow that covered everything was pure white and positively radiant. The footprints I was leaving in it didn't come from anywhere; they simply appeared as if dropped from the sky. It looked magical and I felt like I was living in a fairy tale.

I knew where I would find Kreios. In his library, probably by that eternal fire in the fireplace.

"Kreios," I called out, my own voice coming back to me like music—it was altogether lovely. "Where are you?" I knew precisely where he was. I only called out because it was polite.

When I walked into the library, everything rippled and flickered before my eyes. It was like there were multiple versions of reality that overlapped, and I could see them all at once. It was hard for me to believe, and it triggered a cascade of memories that nearly caused me to stumble.

Kreios was kneeling on the stone floor before the fireplace, hunched over, his hands planted palms down. He was engrossed in a book. More littered the floor around him.

"Kreios."

Looking up, he stood and ran to me, wrapping me up in his arms. "Airel, you are awake—alive." He kissed my cheeks and held me at arm's length, looking me over. "You look well. Better than well—you glow."

I smiled and hugged him again. "I've missed you." The last I'd seen of him, he was about to have a knock-down, drag-out with

Ellie. "Where is Ellie?"

Kreios's face darkened. "Gone. She left again."

I knew better than to press him. "Michael?"

"I was going to leave and find him as soon as my research was complete." He gestured to all the books. "Airel, we may have a plan that will allow us to destroy the Bloodstone."

"What? I thought that wasn't possible."

He hesitated. "You have read my Book. You know where it comes from."

"Yeah. The other side, right? Paradise?"

"These things are not so simple. That is why . . ." Again, he gestured to the books strewn around the room. "I need more information before we can strike well. I need to formulate a strategy."

"How's Michael feel about all this?" I didn't have what I would call a good feeling about it, and something was bothering me about my grandfather. I could smell death on him. I knew he was the Angel of Death—I read the Book, as he said—but this was different. It was death and decay.

"Airel," he said, "Michael is fighting the call. He is the Alexander and next in line to be Seer. What we believe he must do—the only way forward—is high risk."

"I don't like the sound of this. Not at all. Kreios, I . . ." I couldn't hold back the storm of tears. He took my hand and led me to the couch in front of the fire. I buckled and wept. All I could say was, "Mom," over and over again.

At length, he spoke. "I am very sorry, Airel. Your mother was an excellent woman."

"I don't know what happened, I don't know anything—she just died. And Dad's gone, off on business somewhere, which might as well mean he's dead or as good as dead, and I'm . . ." I breathed and sobbed. "I'm trying so hard not to hate him." I collapsed again. I was overwhelmed.

Kreios must have known it needed to happen because he let me get it all out. It took a while. When the grief had subsided, he took my face in his hands. "I know this is hard, but we have to be strong. As hard as it is for me to say this, you are going to have to let him go, Airel. We need you; you are exceptional. Let Michael take care of himself."

I could feel the truth in that statement pummeling my bruised heart. I allowed it to numb me. Numbness was what I needed in order to go on.

Kreios's eyes filled and darkened to obsidian once more, signifying war. "Your life as a teenager is over, Airel. You wield the Sword of Light, you are peculiar, unmatched, the only one of your kind. You have become the supreme Angel of El."

What does that mean?

He responded as if I'd asked it out loud. "That means you are the key."

I've had dreams about this kind of talk. Fear took a stab at me, but something within me that was stronger instantly repelled it.

"Right now we need you, Airel. I need you."

I nodded. I intuited things were beginning to go wrong, though I couldn't get any more specific than that. "What is Michael planning to do?"

Before he even said the words, I knew—I could feel it. "He is going to become the Seer."

KREIOS COULD FEEL IT in his bones more than he could understand it in his mind. His time had come to trade an evil for a greater good. He knew that to muster the army of the damned was against the will of El, against the betterment of mankind, but he had tried every alternative. He did not see any other way to stop to what was happening across the globe.

A global war with the Brotherhood. Such a thing was unprecedented.

Airel was young but strong—much stronger than she believed even now. He took her hand and helped her to her feet. "You must go, Airel. Follow the guidance She will give to you. Lend support to Michael and stop the Brotherhood once and for all. The crowning of the new Seer will draw every member of the Brotherhood; this is the only opportunity we will have to kill them all in a single stroke."

"Why are you talking like you're not coming?" She furrowed her eyebrows, which made him smile.

"I have other matters to attend to, my daughter. But I shall be right behind you, bringing up your rear guard. Do not worry. I shall return—look for me. But do not wait to strike the Brotherhood. You may only get one chance."

She turned from him. "Be safe." She turned back and threw herself into his arms.

He kissed the top of her head. "Go, daughter. Help Michael to remember his love, how much it costs, what it is to fight for what matters. He needs you to show him. Do not give up, Airel. No matter what."

Airel brushed away a tear, nodded, kissed his cheek, and walked out the door. He could hear the sound of the waterfall when she opened the door, and it conjured memories of the first time he'd brought her here. It was another life. She was a child then. "Be well, daughter. Fly true."

Once she was gone, he went to his bedchamber, donning his black tunic. He wrapped a thick leather belt around his waist and pulled on his old black boots, taking hold of the dark sword he had stolen from the hand of a demon thousands of years ago. It was meant to cut and kill angels. It was fitting that it would soon cut demon flesh.

He took one last look around. Then he opened the door to the Threshold.

It was Cain. The mark El had placed on him was prominent on his forehead, red and raw. "We are ready for your command, Kreios, Son of El, Angel of Death."

Kreios closed the door behind him, watching the concrete walls turn to lush and leafy green vegetation. "Muster the army, Cain. The spoils of battle will be the fulfillment of my promise to you."

Cain bowed low and said, "As you command, lord."

The warm air washed over Kreios, reminding him of the scents of paradise. He lifted himself into the air as the Armies of the Damned appeared before him, two hundred thousand strong.

Cain looked up at the ranks. A smile crossed his withered face.

Kreios did not smile—he would permit himself the luxury of a smile once the demon horde had been conscripted into his ranks. Then he should have something to smile about.

CHAPTER III

Mountains of Hijaz, Present Day

LIKE A STONE PILLAR, he stood on Eden's wall, looking
out over the enemy encampment beyond. He had led the Eden
detachment of angelic forces since the Fall and knew a day like this
would come. Just not so soon.

"Your orders?" His right hand said. He wore a gilded helmet
and his breastplate gleamed, his expression communicating interest,
but not a trace of fear.

He shrugged, a glint of sun catching in the chalk-white primary
feathers of his wings. "They do nothing. Days have now passed
with no word of intent." He squinted his eyes and looked at the
details, like a hawk searching for prey. "Not so much as a scout to
ensnare."

"This bothers you much, I can see,"

"Indeed, something is wrong. Why do they wait?"

Another winged soldier arrived and landed lightly on the wall.
"The tree is protected, my lord; our best now guard it in three
contingents. None shall cross the line."

Nodding, he began to pace the wall. The fact that the enemy

had been allowed to get this close to Eden told him much about
the state of the world now. "The thin places must lie in tatters." He
gazed out beyond the trees, past the great river. It was a concern.
"What do you think they are waiting for?" One asked. His
clean-bronzed face was the most boyish of the entire detachment,
and that was saying something. Perhaps what was most striking
about his appearance was that his eyes were so pure. He wondered
how it would feel to lead angels like this into battle, how it would
feel to issue the order that would, for some, and maybe for this one,
mean death. The young one's golden armor shone like the rest of
the Eden guard, but he had never seen battle, and it showed in those
striking eyes.

"I do not know why they wait. Perhaps they await further
orders." He glanced at his troops. "Much like you." But if that was
true, it meant something on the other side had not yet happened,
was not yet aligned. The truth was, the horde army would attack
whenever it was ready to do so. After all, they'd come this far. And
I thought that was impossible. He prayed whatever it was keeping
them encamped would continue to hold them fast. If it came to open
battle, his detachment was outnumbered three to one.

But over time, he had learned how to conceal his thoughts
from the rest, so he hid all his doubt. "We have nothing to fear, my
noble angels. El's Angel of Fire guards the gate night and day with
a flaming sword on every side. None will pass through as long as he
stands."

The man he considered his right hand said nothing. He had
fought many battles, had won some and lost few. He did know he
would take nothing for granted. Not now, as he could see with his
own eyes these black hordes in bold trespass just beyond his walls.
Even the Angel of Fire can be defeated. He dismissed the young
angel and turned back to his old friend. "What is your assessment of

morale?"

"Weak. As if their power is being drained from them, as if—"
He stepped closer and lowered his voice, "as if the demons are
feeding upon it."

He nodded. When the time was right, his troops would be
defenseless. He had to admire the enemy strategy. If it were true.
"Tonight is the new moon. It will be very dark. Send two of your
best to go beyond the trees to the thin place and observe the state
of it. Tell them to see if there are more enemy troops coming. Give
orders that they are to make their way back so they can scout the
enemy camp and report any intelligence they can gather."

"Yes, my lord."

"This waiting does not accrue to our benefit if a battle is to be
fought." He spoke low, to himself. "The longer we wait, the weaker
we get."

Glasgow, Scotland, Present Day

JORDAN WESTON TOOK THE phone call, waving off his
secretary.

It was the assassin, Valac. "I have something you want, Jiki, but
money will not be sufficient this time."

Jordan leaned back in his chair and took a sip of Scotch. He
sounds quite satisfied with himself. "You agreed to a price. The
terms of the arrangement were for cash."

"Oh, we agreed, yes, but the situation has changed now. What
I have is of more value to you than money. I might even call it
priceless."

Jordan sat forward and leaned his elbows on the desk, rubbing the bridge of his nose with his un-good hand. "I am growing tired of these games. What is it you think you have?"

"The heir, the blood of the three. The rightful Seer."

Jordan set his glass down. The demon bluffs—how could he know? Jordan had his sources the world over, but who had Valac been listening to?

"I'm waiting, darling. What's your decision?"

"Is he willing to come with you? Does he know?"

There was a muted sound. "You really have underestimated me. Do you want him, or should I hand him over to that crazy one, old what's-his-name? Kreios? Or maybe I'll kill him and eat him. Better yet, I'll deliver him to the anticherubim. They will kill him for sure, and then we can all be done with the whole thing."

Jordan rubbed his un-good arm. "If you harm him, I will make you yearn for death." He wished Valac were standing right in front of him now. He unleashed a shout of frustration, venting his anger into the office ceiling. The secretary poked her head in with a concerned look on her face, but Jordan shooed her away.

There was laughter coming over the phone line.

"Okay, Valac," he said, his tone cloying and sick. "I will pay whatever you want. Name it. It's yours." The Seer was the only one who could destroy the Tree of Life, and with that Tree still standing, they would never be rid of the cursed Sons of El. The anticherubim and their weak faction believed nothing but that the Alexander was the rightful Seer and they would stop at nothing to see Michael Alexander anointed, whether there really was a blood heir of the line with a prior claim or not.

"I want the stone," Valac said, his voice filled with malice.

"Impossible!"

"That's my new price. You can crown my man as Seer without it. You know that as well as I do, Jiki."

Jordan managed to control his anger, being very careful to keep his tone in check. "Okay, we have a deal. Bring him to the temple of Tengu. You know the place?"

"Of course. I can hear its call even now, same as you. Word that the Seer has been found is beginning to spread; we all gather to see his glory. We're already on our way."

Jordan suppressed a growl. "Good. I will meet you there. Keep him safe; do not let any harm come to him."

"I will protect him with my life."

Jordan slammed the phone down and called for his secretary. She sauntered in and sat on his desk. "You called for me, boss?" She reached out and fiddled with the handkerchief in his breast pocket.

He poured himself a lowball of Scotch, flooding it all the way to the brim. "Get the pilot on the phone and tell him to file a flight plan for Dubai immediately."

"Yes, sir," she said. "Anything else?"

He chugged the whisky and slammed the glass down. "Yeah. How about you pack yourself a bag. It's a long flight, and I'll need a snack."

She giggled and scampered out. She didn't know how literally he meant that.

But as soon as she closed the door behind her, he had guests. Unwelcome ones. The kind that come right out of the walls.

THERE WERE ONLY TWO anticherubim twitching and jerking around in Jordan Weston's office. He wondered offhand where the other one was.

At length, they settled enough to speak, but Jordan could not understand them until he shifted into his alter ego, Jikininki.

Theirs was the old language, one he could not understand as Jordan Weston.

"We called the Alexander and hunted the assassin Valac, but he has escaped us."

"Well done, idiots."

They ignored him. "We need the Bloodstone. You promised it to us."

Jiki did not have time for this—he had a flight to catch. "You two were sent to help with the upcoming war, but so far all you do is get in the way."

"You betray us? Do you dare to change the terms of our arrangement?"

"Why not? That kind of thing is going around lately," he said, mostly to himself. "No matter. The Alexander is so much wind. He wrestles against the power of the Bloodstone; he harbors love in his heart. He is no longer needed."

The bigger one growled. "We only ascribe honor to the blood line of the Alexander. All others are fraudulent. You speak of the Other. The Prince will not accept him. Give us the Bloodstone. We are able to convince the boy Alexander."

This pus-bedecked, fungus-laden demon now confirmed his suspicions. The Prince wants the Bloodstone as well as full control of the Brotherhood. Jordan had hoped to avoid all-out war over the Bloodstone, but it seemed pointless now.

"The Bloodstone will be at the temple of Tengu for the anointing of the new Seer. The Bloodstone will either choose him or it will reject him. Which, I cannot say."

The demons twitched and convulsed back and forth continually, flitting about the room as if holding still would kill them. "You refuse the Prince?"

"I honor the Heir. The rest is politics." Jiki turned his back to them. "The Prince was supposed to destroy Kreios and his halfbreed spawn, Airel. He was powerless to do so. Now I must do it for him."

"The Angel Kreios lives under El's protection."

Jiki laughed. "Are you saying you are powerless to kill him? Is he is beyond your reach too? I thought the legendary three of the original kind were the right hand of the Prince, yet you cannot even bring me the Bloodstone. You need a little half-dead demigod like me to do it for you."

"You mock the Prince and your lords. Remember whom you serve, Jiki."

Jiki paused in thought. "I only want to see the true Seer anointed. If the Alexander can be convinced, as you say, then I propose an arrangement."

"We are listening."

Jordan smiled. "Bring the boy to me now and we will anoint him together. If he is accepted, I will pledge my loyalty to him, but if not—"

"He will be accepted," the two said in unison.

"Very well."

"When we come, you must have the Bloodstone in your possession, or you shall pay for your error with your life."

"Agreed." They left and he switched back into his human garments, his walking-around-town suit of clothes. He chortled. "I shall enjoy watching you try."

Soon he was seated comfortably in his subsonic business jet with his secretary giving him that look she liked to give. He smiled back wickedly as they rolled for takeoff.

CHAPTER IV

Dubai, UAE, Present Day

JOHN CROSS HUGGED HIS old friend Ethan Maxwell, noticing that he was still in impeccable shape if a little bushier around the eyebrows. "How are you, Ethan?"

Holding John out at arm's length, he grinned. "Right as rain, Johnny boy. It is truly good to see you, my old friend. You should bring the family here. I'd love to see them—"

John hoped he wouldn't have to explain the awkward details about how his daughter was in a coma and his sweet Maggie was a shell of herself at Airel's bedside, but Ethan never stopped to take a breath.

"Oh wait, I don't exist. I forgot." Ethan jabbed him. "Must be all the killing and dying." He threw his head back and laughed.

John smiled reflexively. "You do exist, but you're also dead, so . . ."

"I love being dead," Ethan said. "No constraints. You should try it sometime."

John laughed again. It was insincere, but to men like Ethan, that didn't matter a whit. "Maybe I will."

"Maybe you should, Johnny boy. Now. First, how dare you show up without calling. What if I had a woman here? It would have been embarrassing."

"Really?"

"Well—for you." Ethan laughed again. The apartment was lavish, a studded glass jewel high up in an exclusive tower that overlooked the sea on one side and the city lights on the other.

John said, "I've walked in on you in worse situations. Remember Shenyang?"

"You never knew how to have fun."

"They were underage."

"Barely. And technically not, according to some of the lesser-known procedures within the Chinese government." He waggled a finger at him, turned away, and pulled a couple of beers from the fridge.

John would have been surprised at Ethan's lowbrow approach to hosting if he didn't know him better. Ethan Maxwell, once a regular guy from Schenectady, never learned how to care about genteel behaviors. He didn't do couth, he didn't drink aristocratic alcohol, and he didn't give two rips about what anyone thought about any of it. He occupied a special place in John's heart and mind because John was his junior partner when he first came on at the CIA. They worked together for years; Ethan was his mentor. If there was anyone John felt like he could trust, it was this man.

Ethan knew more about John than Maggie did. He knew about the nightmares early on—stuff he didn't dare tell anyone else. Ethan was there in D.C. when he'd first met Maggie; he'd practically introduced them. Ethan and John smoked cigars when Airel was born. They never got together for barbecues and the like because Ethan was a womanizing world traveler based out of D.C. and John was . . . well, John is just John.

A moment passed in silence. "Why so quiet? You came a long way for a drink."

"You crack open a good can of beer, Ethan."

He chuckled. "That I do, that I do. Now, before you start to bore me to death, tell me what you want, and remember, I'm old now. I'm not up for the midnight kill-and-drag thing anymore. I run the big stuff now."

John decided to tell him the truth. Up to this very moment, he was going to give Ethan a story, get what he needed, and go. He watched the fountain in the corner of the room, letting his mind get lost in the sound of water moving, rushing, trickling. It had the same effect as fire; it could hypnotize, it held power. It was seductive.

"Airel is in a coma."

Ethan was silent, looking away.

"Maggie just sits there at her bedside, empty. Waiting."

"I'm sorry for that, Johnny boy. I really am. What else ails you?"

John took the hint. Ethan was the opposite of sentimental. "Ethan, I've managed to get myself into something big. Something I can't control." He let it all hang out with an even, steady voice, no emotion, not once looking away from the fountain.

"Go on."

"I came up with some big debts after South Africa."

"I saw that. You pulled some big levers getting out of there unscathed."

"Tell me about it. That's how MAGICIAN found me." John searched his eyes for a trigger of recognition, but it wasn't there. Besides, Ethan was better than that. "I was given a dead-end job in Glasgow, and by the time I got back home, I was a marked man."

"How so?"

"They're hunting me."

"Who?"

"You wouldn't believe it if you saw it. I have two rotting bodies in my house, Ethan. Neither one is human. Do you believe in demons?"

Ethan laughed but said nothing further.

John reached into his briefcase, took out the book, and placed it on the counter. "And there's this. Volume III of a set of books about an organization called the Brotherhood. They're demons. No kidding. I found it under my daughter's mattress. It seems to be very old. I think the two monsters I killed wanted it, and wanted to kill me to get it."

"Monsters?"

"Ethan, you know me."

He reached for the book. "May I?"

John nodded sliding the book toward him. Ethan flipped through it, making small sighs and grunting noises. After John was done with his drink, Ethan closed the book and took out a bottle of eighteen-year-old Balvenie Scotch and set it on the table between them.

"You? And Scotch? Really?"

"People change, buddy." Ethan grabbed some glasses and began pouring. "Especially when the stress begins to mount."

John smirked. "You think you know a guy."

"Hey. It's the end of the world out there. I believe you, John. You're not the guy to come all the way to Dubai just to tell lies to his oldest and best friend. This story is so strange, it has to be real."

John nodded.

"Johnny boy, I'm not really into this kind of stuff. But . . . I may know someone who is. His name is Jordan Weston. I ran across him a few years back on a job—the details don't matter to you, boy, but he's in to rare books and he's always talking about the end of the world and staring out the window." He laughed, but for the first time, it showed the strain that was now becoming self-evident. He snapped out of it. "Anyway, he was in the market for a book like this. And there was a stone of some sort too, if I remember right."

"I may have helped him."

"What?"

"Yeah, MAGICIAN. I think that may have been Weston. I was supposed to take down this mark in Scotland and grab a stone off her. It's in this book. At least I think it is. It's called the Bloodstone. Some sort of magical trinket the Brotherhood wants."

"Well, well, well. All roads lead to Rome, huh?" Ethan snapped the book shut and set it down.

"Yeah, something like that. So where can I find this Jordan guy?"

"I don't know. I know some of his haunts. And I share some, not all, of his . . . enthusiasms, let's say. I'll check in with my little birds. Hang on." Ethan took up his phone and began tapping away.

"What, right now?"

"Yeah, Johnny boy. You have friends in high places now."

John got up and paced the room. He found the view from the top of the world to be intoxicating. I wonder why I chased after Maggie. I wonder why I chased after that whole life—the house, the job, the PTA, the sensible cars and the grocery-getting monotony of it all. He found himself making arguments pro and con inside the space of his own head, wondering at the amorality of a gun smuggler now having second thoughts about his suburban life and sweet little suburban wife. He thought about how convenient it was that Airel was in a coma now, how she would probably die, how Maggie would no doubt follow her soon after, and how that would free him up to—well, to live a life more like Ethan's. Sleek, proud, a self-proclaimed master of the universe. Money to burn.

"All right, Johnny boy. My birdies tell me Jordan Weston
has something big planned. I personally would like to watch, in a
manner of speaking. His office is at the Burj downtown. I'll get you
his floor number; that should be all you'll need."

"Thanks."

"Sure thing. Johnny . . . Be careful. This isn't the standard deal
we used to run. This is something different."

John's mind ran wild. "But they tried to kill me."

"So you're what, gonna run straight for the viper's nest?"

"I want answers."

Ethan cocked his head and raised his shaggy eyebrows. "You'll
get more than you bargained for, I'd wager."

"Yeah, well. Don't bet on the house this time."

Ethan exhaled, the sound incredulous. "Have another drink.
You're gonna need it. It's strange goings on, John. This earthquake,
the blackouts, and now all the missing people."

"What missing people?"

Ethan placed his hands on the cold granite countertop. "People
all over the place are disappearing. Poof, up and gone, except
there's this weird red residue, sticky and weird. Some say it's that
Christian thing—the Rapture, people disappearing. Some say
it's like the fingerprint of a person's soul. Scientists say they've
discovered a new element—one that's alive."

"What? How come I've never heard this?"

"There's no such thing as news anymore, John. Dubai and
Stockholm are the last two safe places on earth. Everything else has
been plunged into the Dark Ages, Part II. I know because I have
birdies. The world is falling apart, John. This red soul dust—it's
alive. And worse, it can't be killed."

"What?"

"People tell me there's an army being forged in the underworld.

Souls, John. Things are out of order. I have a feeling that book there," he gestured with his glass, "and this Bloodstone thing . . . they're the reason why."

CHAPTER V

DRESSED APPROPRIATELY IN A hooded black cloak, Michael Alexander crossed over to Dubai using the Threshold. With friends like Kreios, he thought there would come a time when impossible things ceased to be amazing. Wrong again. Oh, there's a little closet in your church of a bedroom, next to your arsenal of costumes—because everybody has one of those—and it has a door that takes you down the rabbit hole? Sure, I'll buy that. Michael could only think of Airel's snarky comments about Narnia. It brought the smirk back to his face, despite all that had happened.

All that has happened…

He could hear it in his head now, the call of the Bloodstone. His heart felt sick, dark. He remembered when he was last under the influence of the power of the Bloodstone. It was a potent drug. It was overwhelming, beautiful. He had been surprised—he expected to feel different when so intimately connected with the essence of evil. But it wasn't like that—it was raw and alive, no filter, no boundaries, no limits.

But that was then, back when Stanley had been around, back when it was all fun and games. The need he felt inside his body and mind now was not pleasant at all. It was demanding and painful. And whenever he succeeded in shoving aside these dark and forbidding urges, all he could think about was Airel. How artificial and empty she looked, lying there hooked up to tubes and machines. Life was a steady drizzle of tortures.

If I'd never met her, she would be living a normal life right now. She would never have been activated—she would have been happy. There were times when he wondered if he caused more pain than joy.

This is my only chance to make things right. Maybe he would be able to at least put an end to the bloodshed. He could remember the days when he thought killing the halfbreeds was honorable, even right. Stanley had taught him to hate. Guilt was the only logical result for him when he thought of how he had innocently fallen in love with Airel only to find out he'd been on the wrong side his entire life.

He successfully blocked most of the memories of his kills, but sometimes he would wake suddenly at night and see the dead faces of all his halfbreed kills from years past. He felt he could never repay and never atone for what he'd done, but this—this self-sacrifice—was a start. He could do this—he could give himself up in an effort to try to destroy the Bloodstone. I only hope Kreios can do what he told me he could do, and that he shows up on time.

When he stepped out into the stifling heat that suffocated the sands near Dubai, he knew he was close to where he needed to be. He could feel it. The Threshold read it on his heart and mind, and like a bird flying south for the winter, the part of him that was connected to the Brotherhood knew the location by instinct.

Michael climbed to the top of a sand dune, the wind whipping his face. The great city rose from the ocean like the spine of a great monster, the Burj Khalifa its most prominent feature. Look there.

It's just another tower of Babel. Oh, how he resented all the lies he had bought over the years.

Somewhere beyond the realm of what he could see, he sensed a horde amassing, gathering to witness the anointing of the new Seer. *I won't let you down.* This was in his blood—it was what he was born to do.

"Welcome home, Master Alexander." The voice chattered and spit from behind him, each syllable subdivided into innumerable phlegm-riddled blasts. Michael smiled and turned, and thus began the grand deception.

"We've been waiting for you," they said.

"There are only two of you," he said to the anticherubim. "Where is the other one?"

"Engaged. It matters not. Come with us, master. We will take you to the temple of Tengu."

Michael nodded but said nothing further. He blocked out his mind, focusing with all his power and will upon his role.

I am Michael Alexander, the rightful Seer, blood child of the damned and son of Stanley Alexander. He would not fail, even if it cost him his life.

Boise, Idaho, Present Day

ELLIE STOOD IN THE open doorway in the gathering dusk on the front porch of Airel's house. The door was kicked aside, the lights—those that hadn't been broken—were on, and the place was totally trashed. The looters had come and gone, but as she looked more closely, she could tell there was more going on here than looting. Some of the high-value stuff was left behind, like the television. But the couch was overturned, its cushions denuded of their upholstery, and every drawer in the kitchen was out and spilled in a pile on the floor.

Someone is looking for something.

She unsheathed her sword and made her way through the rest of the house. She could smell Brotherhood stench—demon blood left a pungent odor wherever it was spilled. There was a pile of ash at the top of the stairs right outside Airel's room. Dead Brother. The rest was a stinking hunk of rotting flesh.

She gagged. This one was not a run-of-the-mill demon Brother. It stinks too much. And it hadn't vanished into dust and ash like those did. This one was more hardy than that. It did not need to bond with a person to gain its full strength; this was one of the Original Rebels, a killer, and a hunter.

She went back down the stairs and sat in the broken opening of the front door, breathing air that was not acrid. "What did you boys want here?" she asked, more to hear herself than anything else. She rubbed her chest. The Mark had gone deep, where she couldn't touch it. It was learning. Every hour, it took more of her heart, grasping deeper, binding to her DNA and replicating itself from there at the very foundation of her life. She didn't know how much longer she would last.

She sheathed her sword and tried to think.

What now?

The sun, a cool orange fire, was sinking low in the west. She wondered if she would see it ever again.

What am I? Am I angel, am I Brother, or am I just a girl who's lost her way in life? Am I a victim of circumstance, even after all these years? She was a 2700-year-old grandmother who looked all of maybe nineteen. That was what she was. A walking contradiction. She thought it over and then she took off running up the stairs, to the corpse.

She covered her nose and mouth. The stink was so bad.

I was one of these once, part of the Brotherhood. She knew she had the ability to manipulate kings and princes; she could maybe read the mind of a dead rebel, too. How hard could it be? Opening her mind, she reached into the dead monster's cortex and began looking for answers.

A flood of hijacked memories came at her, fast. They hurt physically. As she fought through the pain, it was difficult to keep abreast of her own identity and not lose herself in the storm. Finally, she pushed off, stumbled back through the hall, tripped in the dust pile of the other one, and fell halfway down the stairs.

She steadied herself and gasped. Now it's coming clearer. She understood why the two assassins were here now. It can't be even remotely true. Or possible. But she had to admit it was the only thing that made any sense.

Part of her wanted to have a moment to weep, but she didn't allow herself the luxury.

She knew where to go now.

She stood up tall, breathed deep, and walked to the front door. She swatted the ash from her jeans before vanishing into the atmosphere.

The anointing of the new Seer was imminent, and she wasn't going to miss the party—every last one of them was going to be there, and there couldn't be many of them left now. It will be like shooting fish in a barrel.

If she lived to see the end of it.

CHAPTER VI

Dubai, UAE, Present Day

JOHN FOUND PIERRE AFTER saying good-bye to Ethan.

They took a car the short distance to the Burj. As they talked, John found it was a small world—the friend in high places Pierre had been talking about all this time was none other than Jordan Weston. So it's two birds with one stone, then. Only John's heart raced, his stomach was in knots, and he had a severe case of heartburn.

Something didn't sit right and John chewed on it all the way to the 144th floor, where he found it still wouldn't go down easy.

John and Pierre cooled their heels in the late-afternoon sun-soaked lounge of a dance club near the top of the world's tallest building, waiting for their appointment.

As was customary in his dealings with Important People, John knew the drill—hurry up and wait; don't speak until spoken to; the first to talk money loses. Despite how much had changed in the world of late, it was alarming at how little change the modus operandi actually had undergone. Money makes the world go 'round, John thought. Always has, always will.

Instead of acknowledging the awkward silence between himself and his newest partner Pierre, instead of doing the slightest thing about it, he sipped green tea from bone china, staring out the windows. John wasn't sure whether to resent or reward him for his connections, so he did nothing.

The door opened. "Mr. Cross." It was the executive assistant. He turned.

"He's ready for you, sir."

"Very well," John said, motioning to Pierre to come along.

Pierre agreed beforehand that he would only make introductions and that John would take over from there. To John, Pierre was mostly here for appearances anyway. In these circles, everyone had people—handlers, assistants, bodyguards, thugs. And John wanted to appear to be "normal", that Pierre was one of his "people". The people he usually dealt with found appearances to be reassuring; appearances drove home the idea that John was the real deal.

They took the elevator farther up, to the 154th floor, and walked out into a clean, modern lobby. There were double doors at the far end. As they approached, those doors opened to reveal a reception area. A wiry man with an earpiece sat behind a high desk.

He motioned to them to be seated.

Of course.

John disciplined himself to keep from rolling his eyes. He shared a glance with Pierre, wordlessly urging him to keep cool. It was a simple power play; they would be made to wait another five to ten minutes.

As John sat, he was briefly overcome by what he might have irritably termed his conscience—it was like taking a too-large dose of medicine. It was a gigantic "what-am-I-doing" glimpse, an alarming whiff of perspective in which he could taste, see, even smell himself exactly as others might be able to do.

It was repellent.

In that split second, as his full weight came to rest on the seat that supported him, he thought of how at one time he had been innocent, back when he was young and ignorant and uncynical. Back when he had been an amorous husband, a plucky optimist new hire, an inexperienced father of a sweet little girl. But it had never felt quite right. He knew somewhere deep down that having a family was wrong for him, though he couldn't put his finger on why. The feeling nagged. He hated that he had to keep so many secrets. His work for the CIA and others had required him to make a completely different life for himself apart from Maggie and Airel.

Ethan was the only one who knew the real truth, that one day he had washed up in South Beach, California, as a John Doe—no ID, no name, no memory. Ethan knew about the nightmares, too. Ethan knew why his name was John—because of standard hospital procedure: John Doe. Ethan was the only one who knew he had no memory of who he was, that when he'd been found and resuscitated, he babbled one word over and over.

Derackson . . . Derackson . . . Derackson.

It was the same word the demon in his house had spoken over him before John had pulled the trigger. John wanted to be able to forget that he had forgotten. By the time he met Maggie, he had perfected the routine to the point where she bought it like it was the truth. John Cross. Pleased to meet you, Maggie. She laughed and asked him if he was a secret agent, and he countered that yeah, he worked for the CIA, but as an accountant.

But everything was a lie. So I'll just keep piling it on, then, he thought. In the end, he did whatever it took to blot out his empty past. He filled the void with lies, with Maggie, with Airel, with all the standard trappings of suburban American life.

They were beckoned onward now by the wiry man with the earpiece.

John got to his feet and took a deep breath. He looked at Pierre. "Ready?"

"Oui, monsieur."

They approached the wiry man, who smiled in plastic. John wondered what lay beneath it, but he didn't wonder too loudly. The door was held open, revealing a sleek and barren room with floor-to-ceiling windows at the far end. A man stood in a tailored suit behind a bar. Beyond those windows was a shallow balcony railed in high-tension cable, on which perhaps a man might be able to pace as he thought about the latest multi-billion-dollar deal.

The man behind the bar introduced himself. "Welcome," he said, clearly talking to Pierre alone, ignoring John as if he were but a servant. He did not move to shake hands. "Cocktail?"

Pierre declined and motioned toward John. "I would like you to meet someone—John Cross. He is searching for a rare book. I thought of you."

John looked around for a place to sit. There was none. Therefore, he stood and faced his host.

Jordan Weston went about his business, making something in a sterling silver shaker and pouring the contents into a glass. The three men stood equidistant from each other, forming a triangle; Jordan with his glass, ice clinking against crystal from within, the other two with their hats still in hand.

John recognized what was happening now—something was about to go down. He had walked right into the middle of a trap.

But than Pierre spoke, rearranging everything. "Come, come, darling. It's time for you to pay up or we'll both walk."

Jordan glared. "You'd never get out alive, Valac."

Pierre shrugged it off and laughed, his eyes yellow and alcoholic now. "Oh?"

For an eternal second, John stood as a reluctant spectator,

looking in on a gunfight. But than Pierre's head twisted around, tearing open in a wet rip, breaking the stifling silence. John watched in horror as the human body fell free and a winged creature unfurled itself. It was half the size of the ones he'd killed in his house, but every bit as much like a dragon. "Behold, Jiki, the Other. Now would be a good time to hand over the Bloodstone so I can be on my way."

Jordan's lack of interest with the demon standing in his office was alarming to John. When their eyes met, Jordan offered a sympathetic smile. "All this is coming as a shock to you, I'm sure. Just give me a moment to wrap up some personal business with our friend here, and then I'll answer all your questions."

Pierre—the demon—laughed, dark slime dripping down its chin. It snapped its jaws at John, making him flinch and cringe. If dragons could laugh, this thing did so. And than the beast gyrated as if beginning a lurid dance, folding inward on itself. When it stood still once more, it had become a teenage boy. The image before John's eyes was familiar to him, even though he was naked. That's the kid Airel went to school with, that Dirk Elliott boy who was all over the news.

"Hey, Mr. Cross. You seen Airel? We had a date, but she never showed up."

John took a step back as the thing moved toward him.

It danced sickly again and recovered into an image of a beautiful redhead with skin like pure cream. "Or does this suit you better, John? We could have a little fun, you and I—"

"Enough," Jordan said.

The woman arched and hissed, transforming back into the beast. "The Stone, Jiki. Now."

"Come," Jordan said.

The demon obeyed, its gaze locked onto Jordan's hand as it

reached behind the counter.

As the monster drew near, Jordan Weston seized it by the throat, dragging it toward the windows. John didn't know what to do or say. As they approached, one of the large panes slid away, revealing the narrow balcony outside. A blast of air invaded carrying with it the dust and noise of the world.

The demon flapped and clawed at the floor in vain. As Jordan held the demon in his iron grip, John saw that his arm was mostly bone and rotten flesh.

With great power, Jordan Weston flung the demon out over the cable rail into thin air.

John stood staring, feeling the tingle of the moment run its fingers along the full length of his shocked body.

Jordan turned back toward him, smoothing his hair down, and as he did, John could hear laughter. It sounded like a little boy laughing as if playing a game. The window closed and sealed, and in the red light of a smoke-veiled sun, John saw the beast—Pierre, Dirk Elliott, the redhead, the dragon—flying away unharmed.

Jordan Weston's eyes were on fire.

John was a deer in the headlights.

Jordan walked to the bar, drew a breath, and held it. "Where was I, where was I?" He fumbled around a bit with bottles and glasses and then stopped, staring into space. "Ah. Cocktail?" he asked John.

John cleared his throat. "I could use one, if you don't mind."

"Yes, good. I knew you would say that," Jordan said. "After we've had a few drinks, we can talk. You and I have a lot to catch up on, and not much time." He smiled and rubbed his arm, the one that looked to be dead. "And don't worry about Valac. He'll be back, but by the time he regroups, it will be too late."

CHAPTER VII

Mountains of Hijaz, Present Day

THE ANGEL OF EDEN stood like a tower of bronze as the Eden Detachment gathered near him on the garden wall. The air was taut. The Brotherhood horde had finally mobilized. Men and demons chanted in withering black speech as they approached, and yet the angelic host waited for their captain to issue orders. The wall of Eden could withstand any army. Although they were outnumbered, they were still blessed by the power of El.

Even so, he could feel it wane, and he knew his men could too. Time had run out.

Flame burst from below as the Angel of Fire engaged the front line of the Brotherhood advance.

"Fly," he whispered, and like a storm, the angels poured down from the wall, loosing a hail of spears and arrows. Blades of swords and axes hacked and crashed into the black fog of membranous wings and foul flesh below.

He could feel now more than ever the power in the drain. The Brotherhood was sucking him and his forces dry. He drew his sword and dropped into the melee. The sounds of close battle were unmatched. It had been millennia since he had drawn cold steel in anger. He looked around for the young one as he hacked through talons and scraping swords, men dying. He saw him in the distance, flying in great loops as he had been trained, striking parallel to enemy lines, flanking them, taking ten or more at a time. Good boy. To his other side, he beheld one of his other old guard, removing enemy heads with the two-bitted battle axe, flying, spinning, hacking at demon flesh like a harvester. Men and beasts were thrust through with angel blades, and there was the sound of bones breaking, grist in the mill. There was no music as terrible as this. There was no mere talk. There was only death's threshing floor, and these honorable Defenders of Eden were the winnowing fork.

But than a giant white demon, chalked and enrobed in mossy tangles of decay, came forth from the enemy ranks. Each of its hands was like the branches of a great dead and fruitless tree. It advanced and stood face-to face-with the Angel of Fire.

Right at the Gate.

He watched as fire subsumed the angel's form, shielding him and blinding his foes. "Get back!" he commanded his men, giving the Guardian of the Gate of Eden ample space to maneuver.

The Angel of Fire swelled with a flourish, a great heavenly sword in each hand, coming to his ready position.

The giant demon took hold of his prey and tore it in half.

The hope of victory abandoned him as he watched the most powerful of Eden's angels become snuffed like a wet wick. El, where is the help we were promised?

He dodged a slashing tail and flew toward the giant white demon.

It turned toward him, looking bored.

Is there no end to evil? Every death of the Eden Detachment was relayed to his mind; he could feel every death. The young

one and his old friend might still be fighting, but exhaustion
was pounding in on all of them. It was no use; they would stand
guarding the Tree, and he would be the last to die defending it. It
was better this way, to die doing what they were created to do.

"You need not die, Captain of El," the giant white demon spoke,
its voice like the rasp of dead leaves in a cold wind. "Show us the
Tree and we will let you live."

Eden was a place of many secrets. "I will never surrender the
Tree or Eden."

"I will rip it up by the roots; you shall watch me do it." It
kicked the flaming corpse of the Angel of Fire as it stepped toward
him, flicking his sword away and laughing.

He flew a little higher and circled around, searching for his
soldiers. He called out for his old friend and heard nothing. The
young one was now gone, he was sure. He didn't want to admit it,
but they were all gone. Now there was no denying it—the Eden
Detachment was lost. The noises of the battle drew to a quiet, and
he could feel only the remnant of the six who stood in guard around
the Tree.

"Still believe in your God?" The white demon snatched him out
of the air by the neck and lifted him high as a trophy for his horde to
behold. They greeted the white demon with a cheer, holding up their
dead in response. It turned back to him. "Where is your God now?"

El, help me. He was so weak, he couldn't answer his captor. He
stared across the mass of men and demons, at the broken bodies of
his soldiers, and prayed for mercy.

But none came. The gates were broken down, and he was
powerless to do anything but watch as the Brotherhood stormed into
Eden.

But they did not get far.

Just inside the gate, his captor spun, crouched, and growled low.

He then saw what the rest of the horde army saw—a blaze of white speeding toward them.

"What is this?" the white demon said.

It was Kreios. With thousands of the damned in his wake.

The white demon cursed tossing him aside. "Kreios!"

Above the Gate of Eden, the lines were drawn in the sky. Kreios and Cain stood at the front of the Host of the Damned, an army of warriors who couldn't be vanquished by any but the word of El. Opposite these was the invasion force of the Brotherhood.

The white demon spoke. "You can see with your own eyes that I have already won, Kreios." It sniffed the air. "And I do not sense the Sword of Light in your possession. What brings you to this battle hoping for victory, Kreios the Fallen? Kreios the Rebel?" There was Brotherhood laughter at this taunt.

Kreios the Angel of Death glowed blue around the markings of his neck and arms. "Asmodeus, you will not see the sun of another day. I came for your Nri Brothers. And now I come for you. It is time to make an end of your kind once and for all."

CHAPTER VIII

Dubai, UAE, Present Day

JOHN COULD HEAR SOMETHING in his head, feel a presence. It made the hair of his arms prickle. They had descended four floors to the 150th of the Burj, where a door opened onto the rear of an auditorium. He stepped inside as Jordan Weston held the door and smiled. The far wall was a bank of windows, and the room was empty except for a small pedestal under lights in the middle.

"What is this?" John was loose now. He had pounded those drinks down too quickly, and he regretted it. He had come here for answers to questions, but now he wondered what price revelation would exact in exchange.

Jordan's eyebrows came together. "You know what it is, John. I suspect a part of your mind has always known."

John stared at the red stone hovering above the pedestal as it moved slowly in a pool of red light. His next words were instinctual--his conscious mind did not exercise control over them. "The Bloodstone," he whispered.

"Yes."

Jordan's confirmation felt like a judge's sentence being read out, and John found in deep, dormant parts of himself a quickening. It was like a broken part of him had been stitched together and jump started, pulling over him a shroud of black smoke.

"It's the key to everything I've spent my life trying to build," Jordan said. "It's the reason you're here. John, haven't you always felt as if there's been something missing?"

John nodded, his wide eyes locked onto the stone.

"Well, this is the missing piece. Don't you long more than anything to put an end to the mystery of who you are, who you were meant to be?"

"But that's not why I'm here." John saw a shadow move past the large windows that overlooked the city of Dubai. Another shadow dropped from the top to the bottom, like an insect. Then more. It's a swarm. Demons.

Jordan put his good hand on his shoulder. "They're here for you, to witness the anointing of the new Seer."

"What is this—who are you, and what does this have to do with me? I'm just here to find out about . . . about . . ." John wanted to both fall asleep and run from this place all at once. Evil, palpable, simple and clear was what this man represented, and in his eyes John beheld naked and undisguised the pit of all darkness.

But it wore a salesman's smile. "You still don't remember?" Jordan edged his way nearer the Bloodstone, his hand reaching out, but he held back. Fear and longing flooded his face, and he closed his eyes as if in prayer.

John made a play at resistance one last time. He knew it would be his last. "I'm not here for that." As he uttered the last word, his life of lies, a house of cards, crashed in on itself and lay flat, burying under its paper slabs every care he ever had. There was a wife, there was a daughter somewhere in the distant dark mists, but they were irrelevant.

"You were drawn here by the Bloodstone, John Derackson. It is yours to have, yours to hold." Jordan licked his lips, and in the gesture John could see—and he began to feed on—the delicious surrender to the clean nothingness of the inevitable.

The door burst open from behind. Curses broke John from his stupefaction partway. He glanced back to see two thin, winged creatures like fungus-covered skeletons flit into the room. These were followed by a young man he felt like he recognized, but he couldn't put a name with the face yet. The creatures spoke simultaneously. "What is the meaning of this, Jiki? You lied to us."

There's that name again—I wonder what it means. John smiled as if drunk, but his mind was clearing up. The simple facts were becoming obvious. He moved toward the Bloodstone.

Jordan's voice wore the sound of a smile. "Calm yourselves. I have upheld the terms of our arrangement. The Seer will be chosen, just as you wanted."

John searched his mind for information about the young man. The depths of his thoughts were dark, hemmed in by evil memories of enemies, stumbling blocks he had never been quite able to cast off. Until now. There was a name at the peak of these hindrances, and it was bathed in hideous blue—Airel. He roared in rage, trying to shrug it off. With clenched fists and teeth, he turned toward the young man and spoke his name. "Michael Alexander."

"Mr. Cross."

John bristled once more. It was like he was being mocked. And then he corrected the young man. "Not Cross. Derakhshan."

ELLIE REFORMED ON TOP of a skyscraper overlooking downtown Dubai and scanned the sky. A dark cloud covered the top half of the Burj Khalifa. She took a second look when the nature of the cloud mass flexed and moved like a school of fish. It was the Brotherhood in full force, swarming the tower, howling and chanting. *The Seer is here—or soon will be, if I don't hurry.* She took a few breaths. "Guess I know where to go."

She reached out for Kreios but felt nothing. She thought of petitioning El, but her heart was divided. The Brotherhood had gathered here just as she had imagined they would, but their numbers were so much greater than she thought they could be. "What are you getting yourself into this time, Ellie?"

Shadowing herself, she took to the air and headed toward the huge tower that stood over the rest of the city like a spike of silver reaching into the sky. Could she get past the swarm and inside to find Michael? He was sure to be in the middle of it all, whether it cost him his life or not. *I can relate to those kinds of desperate measures,* she thought. Her life had been nothing if not a desperate chain of stumbles. Whatever Michael and Kreios had planned would surely be no match for what she saw before her now.

The Brotherhood had been busy. *They are now truly beyond number.* For the first time in a long time, Ellie found herself afraid.

CHAPTER IX

Somewhere over the North Atlantic Ocean, Present Day

I KNEW ONE THING as I flew across the ocean—it was all
Michael. This was about him and me. It was about how I loved
him, how he had saved my life, even though writing in my book
was forbidden. Love compelled us to do things we might never
ordinarily do, and sometimes the results we got were unexpected
or even wrong. The simple fact was that my life was out of order. I
was here and I wasn't supposed to be. I'm not supposed to be alive.
My out-of-order life was the thing that was causing all the pain and
death in my life. But I knew what I had to do to begin making it
right.

The Brotherhood was now close; I could feel their drain. I drew
the Sword of Light and pushed harder, my signature pure-blue light
trail stretching out behind for miles.

Michael and I were connected now, connected forever, for
better or for worse. He had loved me and risked everything for
me. He had lost his father, turned his back on everything he'd ever
known, and he continued to risk his life for the greater good. Now
I had to do whatever it took to save him from having to give up his

life to protect me.

My mission was simple: Destroy the Brotherhood once and for all.

Might I fail? That didn't matter. With the Sword of Light in my hand, the only thing I knew was that the enemy hadn't yet been able to produce a foe to equal what was possible in me when I wielded this weapon. But there was more. I felt something stirring deep inside me, and it felt like it was about to boil over. The truth was, I had never truly let go and allowed myself to run wild in battle.

It was time to raise all I had to give to El—the white flag of surrender. I would now be Airel, daughter of Kreios, Son of El, Angel of Death.

Immediately as I did, I felt a change. The heavenly Host are coming.

JOHN COULD HEAR CURSES billowing inside his headspace. The Bloodstone pressed his soul; he found himself getting lost in its red light.

He was vaguely aware of the growing crowd of men and demons, but as he gave in to the raw power he felt overcoming him, he moved closer to the Bloodstone.

"Come to me, son." It was inside his head now. "You will find peace and power beyond your imagination. Touch the stone and behold what you seek. Answers will give themselves willingly now . . . Come to me."

MICHAEL BECAME ALARMED. THE situation was degrading

fast. His plan had banked on the assumption that his anointing
would be mostly ceremonial, that the Seer's cloak was his to deny.
But now he looked for a place to hide, and mainly because of the
look on John's face.

Black winged demons filled the room and a low hum resonated
in his head as chanting filled his ears. Something shoved him
forward.

The Bloodstone called to him. "My son. Surrender to me. I am
your rightful father. You can be with Airel forever with the power
I offer you. Come and touch me. I will make you a hero. Airel will
love you forever for that. She will see you as you have always
longed to be seen. Set all those other failures aside and come to me
now."

Michael fought against the pull though he longed to give in to
it more than anything. It was so beautiful, so pure! But he knew all
about these parlor tricks. It was a manipulative ploy. "No," he said,
but his voice was drowned out by the hum, by the chanting.

John was transformed. Michael had never seen someone so
changed by the Brotherhood drain; he brooded over its red light.

The anticherubim were even more skittish than usual, and they
showed it by shoving Michael ever harder toward the Stone. Echoes
of the Original Tongue sounded off as the anticherubim argued with
the other man in the room. Michael wasn't sure who he was, but
they called him Jiki, and he thought of him as John's sponsor.

This was a development he hadn't planned for—the competing
factious clans. He kicked himself that he should have known better
than to walk into a hornet's nest as the Alexander, the presumptive
heir to the Bloodstone. I hope Airel and Kreios get here soon, and
that they have the numbers or the power to make this go our way.
He didn't know what to do.

The man they called Jiki growled and bared his teeth at the

anticherubim and Michael saw that his mouth was filled with rotten, bloody fangs. The anticherubim snarled right back, shoving Michael forward. Jiki pushed one of them and it lunged for him, pulling him down so fast that Michael lost sight of them in the press of the horde for a split second.

There was another snarl, and the struggling pair crashed into the floor at Michael's feet. The anticherubim reached up to Jiki's head, gripped it in its thin arms, and ripped it from his body. Dark blood pulsed from the stump of Jiki's neck. The demon stood and tossed it aside like a useless stone.

Michael stood in stunned silence.

The two anticherubim fell on the body, devouring it with savagery. The chanting increased, and now the mass of people and demons moved back and forth with its rhythm.

Michael averted his gaze and saw John reaching for the Bloodstone. "It is time." He heard the voice of the Bloodstone in his head. "You have been rejected, Michael Alexander."

A blinding red light exploded through the room. Michael was tossed aside into a wall. The darkness was total and the building shook as every man and demon in the ranks of the Brotherhood roared in adulation and victory. The new Seer's time had come.

CHAPTER X

ELLIE MOVED UP THROUGH floor after floor, reforming just in time to see Airel's father reach out and touch the Bloodstone. Michael was nearby, one hand extended, horror on his face. The room was packed solid with chanting Brotherhood generals and key members. Some she recognized. Others were new to her.

But Airel's father, the man whose name was John Cross, was not new. He was no longer a mystery, no longer an unknown quantity. The hijacked memories of the dead rebel from Airel's house came pounding back through her, storming roughshod over what hopeful doubts she had cultivated. Now that she saw him with opened eyes, she knew who he really was.

She rushed toward him to keep him from touching the cursed Stone. But she was too late. Everything went red-dark, and the shockwave threw her across the room.

She righted herself against the back wall at the feet of the jubilant demon horde, pleading with El that she hadn't struggled all these years, that she hadn't come all this way, that she hadn't gotten here only to have run out of time, only to be a witness to the ultimate atrocity. She cried out to her only son, Qiel—the Seer.

I PAUSED HIGH ABOVE the desert, the Sword of Light drawn and ready in my hand. Blackness enveloped the city of Dubai below. The Brotherhood moved like locusts, covering every inch of land, leaving nothing in their wake. The ocean surged over its beaches, and weird waterspouts sprang up from it in tendrils that reached and grasped like animals.

A part of me knew I should be scared. But I wouldn't let myself give into my fear. I didn't care that I was alone, that it was total insanity to even be here. I was going to kill every last member of the Brotherhood or die trying.

I reached out to Kreios, knowing he was far away but still hoping he could hear me. I could use your help. Come as soon as you can.

She filled me with hope and confidence, and for once, we had nothing to say to each other. As I considered my opening move, I saw a wave two miles out to sea begin to swell. It gathered more and more energy as it moved inland.

The Palm—a manmade set of islands—ceased to exist. The tsunami surge consumed everything. Dry ground farther inland cracked open and water poured upward, flooding streets and crumbling the foundations of many buildings as I hovered overhead.

I had never seen anything like it.

But I had read about it. This can only be the work of Qiel, but he's dead. Or missing. This was a pretty big assumption, I realized. The Book of Kreios had revealed no information to me about Qiel after the fall of Ke'elei.

It looked like I had our work cut out for me.

El? A calm overtook me and then I looked, and I saw the first wave of the angelic host army descending. They peeled off on trajectories of white, streaking toward the battle. It was time.

JOHN COULD STILL HEAR the chanting voices of demons, a language which he now understood. He wasn't sure if he understood it for the first time or if he was beginning to understand it again. They called him master, Seer, lord. His mind atrophied as the stone took over his every thought.

He closed his eyes and his fingers around all the facets of the stone. He allowed the voice to probe deep within. He surrendered everything to it.

There was a beach. It was years ago. Bright sun overhead. The surf rushing in again and again, like the hand of a lover awakening him to the dawn of a new day.

He took his first breath in thousands of years. He opened his eyes.

There were paramedics. An ambulance. A hospital room and bright lights, and he chanted the same word over and over again.

"Derakhshan."

"Derakhshan."

"Derakhshan."

It was his mother. He was calling for his mother.

The staff listed his name as John (Doe) Derackson upon release.

Before that, though, was the stone.

The memories came over him in a new wave as the stone unlocked the secrets of his past. He stood in a tent with a sniveling man. The name "Piankhy" came to him, as did the word "General". Yes, I have been Seer before . . . John (Doe) Derackson Cross, eyes closed, breathed. He waited for the vision to augment once more.

More—give me more.

Then it shifted. He saw himself touching the stone, saw Piankhy wrap the chain around his neck, saw as the delicious darkness welled up from beneath his body and took him.

He saw the shadow of his mother, Uriel, the Derakhshan, how she passed by him as she got free of the Bloodstone. Free? Why would anyone want to be free from this?

But then the stone showed him what he did next, and he was ashamed.

He fled.

His first act as Seer was to try to drown himself in the sea. But Qiel could not drown. He took the stone down and down, deep under the deep, lodging himself and the stone within the dark, cold mud of the sea floor. His act of cowardice. The price, as he went to sleep, was losing his memory as the Bloodstone consumed his mind and soul. He was then dormant, the rightful Seer in exile, the Bloodstone cut off from the Brotherhood, the ranks of the rebels in disarray for thousands of years.

The stone had known his plan all along. It did not suffer surprise. And it finally had Qiel, the one it had longed to possess, in its clutches.

But the chain that bound him to the stone rotted and rusted, and soon it was cut off. It allowed itself to be discovered by a seafaring host, and that privateer captain's demon Brother was Tengu, the Bloodstone's former master. The Bloodstone waited for centuries. Then the line of the seafarers was cast off by Tengu in favor of another, and the line of the Alexander was forged. A splint, a bandage. A temporary measure. The Alexander could only ever be a stand-in for the true heir to the power of the Bloodstone.

Only Qiel, son of the runaway Uriel, the Derakhshan, the half-breed daughter of the Angel Kreios, Son of El, Angel of Death, could wield the power the Stone craved. Only Qiel, uniquely powerful and equal parts Brother, angel, and man, could unite the Brotherhood with the Sons of El, or indeed, destroy the rebellion once and for all.

The stone and the power of the prince who laid claim to it bided all time in anticipation of the moment when the truth could finally be revealed. Before the seafarers, before the Alexander, before currents and the vicissitudes of time cut off the Bloodstone from its true host, while Qiel lay in stasis under the oceans, the stone wormed its way deep inside his heart, deep inside his mind. There it pricked his conscience, there it had begun the bloodletting, and there it had bonded with Qiel's very blood.

"It's in your blood, Derackson." A laugh resounded, but he couldn't tell if it was in his head or if it was not. "It's in my blood." Qiel—the only Seer bound by blood to the Bloodstone.

Calm washed over him. When he opened his eyes, the lights in the auditorium flickered on, illuminating the room. Demon Brothers and men scrambled to bow to him, muttering their prayers. Qiel looked down to see that his shirt had become torn and filthy. It hung over his body like a rag. He tore it off and gloried at how his skin glowed with youthful vibrancy once more. Muscles rippled under the skin of his arms. The power surging through him from the deep brought a smile to his lips.

"Qiel." A small voice called to him.

He turned to behold his mother. She was standing before him with flickers of hope and confusion running across her features. "Mother." Qiel betrayed no emotion.

He watched as tears streamed down her face. The witnesses parted and she walked on unsteady feet toward him. "I thought you were . . . I thought . . . my son..." She reached to embrace him, and he opened his arms. She sobbed into his neck, tears trickling down his chest.

In one swift move, Qiel pushed Uriel away and yanked the sword from its sheath that hung at her hip. "I do hope you are ready to die," he said, and without hesitation stabbed the bloody blade deep into her belly. "Ah. There it is. The Mark." He worked the blade in deeper, drawing up.

Blood poured out like water as she fell to her knees. Her mouth swung wide and empty. Qiel didn't wait for her to find any more words. He heaved the blade free and swung it, decapitating her with her own sword.

A roar ensued and the building shook again, the demons swarming over its skin and fouling the air, beating their chests and issuing their war cry.

"Her debt is now paid. She will not betray again."

Another ground-shaking roar.

"Brothers, the time has come. We now rid the world of the weak. Those who belong to El." He called forth the great deeps. He would finish with Airel. She was the daughter he never wanted to have, the offspring who never was, the one person who should never have been born.

CHAPTER XI

CREATURES EMERGED FROM THE ocean that now covered the ground below. Skyscrapers leaned and toppled over, and demons attacked the city and its inhabitants with a newfound fury. Like a beacon in the gathering storm, the silver tower gleamed in the setting sun.

There were now many angels flying into the melee. Some of them picked off hundreds of dark warriors, drawing them out away from the tower. Others plunged straight into the darkness. Most of those did not come back out again.

Come on, girlie. Master your fears.

I flew straight down into a thick cloud of demons and hacked a dozen of them in half before anyone of them noticed I was even there.

As I circled back around, though, I had their attention. They converged on me. The beauty of being small and fighting an enemy that's bigger and strong in numbers is that it's hard to miss your opponent.

Light pouring from the Sword of Light blinded my foes. I dodged a huge paw and severed a head from its owner. I could feel my heart begin to open, to let go, but something still hid there. I wanted to let it all out, to be free at last, to allow El to work through me unhindered.

Why do I still hold back?

Something swatted me. I tumbled end over end and the wind left my lungs. I righted myself and crossed swords with a slender red devil. I made him follow me, dropping like a stone from the sky. I turned, rolled, and looped back, buzzing close, dragging my Sword through his belly. He disintegrated into ash. I cut the wings from two others on my way up, breaking free above the battle.

Howls echoed below, darkness crawled toward me, crackling like a thunderstorm. I could feel the power building inside me as I circled the raging storm of the Brotherhood. They flew in circles trying to keep up, but soon they retreated to a hover as I flew, enclosing a few thousand inside the globe of my light trail.

Time to see what I can do when I let go.

I coasted to a stall and turned toward my prey, hovering. Both hands on the Sword, I leveled it at them and, breathing out, finally gave myself over completely to the will of El. An explosion of light erupted through the odd-shaped hole in the hilt of the Sword. I didn't know at first whether it had come from the Sword or not. But as I looked down, I found my heart glowing in electric blue in the cooling power of the aftereffects. Thousands of demons instantly turned to ash. My power and energy doubled with the discharge. "You are drawing energy from them through the Sword," She said. "The more you kill, the stronger you will become."

Maybe that's the function of the hole in the Sword . . .

But my small victory was short-lived.

A huge winged demon broke free from the swarm around the tall silver tower. Its wings spanned the late-evening sky, dwarfing the other demons. Fear tried to rake my mind, but I would not allow myself to be ruled by it.

Thick fangs protruded from its lower lip like spears sticking out of the ground. Two horns curved from the side of its head, their sharpened tips pointing upward. Scales lined its body, a hard armor covering.

I dodged low and it roared as it flew over me. The lesser demons scattered to get out of the way of the great beast. It grabbed one in its long-fingered clutches and tossed it into its maw. It was but a snack.

It came circling back around.

I reached for Michael but couldn't sense him anywhere. He has to be inside the tower. That's where the Seer would be. But before I could go investigate for myself, I had to take care of my outdoors business.

The house-sized demon beat its wings, coming closer. It would be a tough one to defeat—my mind raced. As much as I hated the idea that came to my mind, it was the best I could do. The closer I am to that thing, the safer I'll be.

I sighed again, grossed out. "All right, let's get this over with." The mouth of the thing was ten feet wide—difficult to miss. I launched myself right into it.

QIEL, EXULTANT, STOOD OVER the lifeless body of his mother, Uriel.

Michael Alexander came running from the cowardly shadows to sob upon her corpse.

Qiel was past regret. He held the Bloodstone in his hand as the Brotherhood generals robed his body in pure white silk. Pulling the hood over his head, he turned to them. "The half-breed Airel is here, and Kreios is coming. Make ready."

The generals agreed with bows and hushes of praise.

He turned to Michael Alexander. "As for you, boy, this is sedition. Why should I allow you to live?" Qiel crouched and peered into the young man's raw eyes. "No. I shall keep you alive. Kreios and Airel may hold still long enough for me to be able to kill them if they believe you still draw breath." Michael pulled himself up and stood over him. He might have said something, but Qiel flicked the air between them and Michael flew across the room, slamming against the wall and crumpling to the floor, motionless.

Qiel stood and straightened his robes, addressing the generals once more. "Bring me Airel. Alive."

They left carrying the unconscious Michael Alexander with them.

The two anticherubim were the last to be dealt with. They stood over the remains of the body of Jiki, twitching. Qiel read their fear like a cheap book. They had no secure ground on which to stand.

Qiel now knew everything the Bloodstone knew. "Have you word of the Tree? Is it secured?"

"Our sister has not reported to us any change. We know of neither victory nor defeat, master."

"No word is defeat. Victory is the quickest word there is. One never is slow to brag of success." The anticherubim had backed the wrong horse. "What's to be done with you, my pretties? My traitorous pretty pets?" Qiel ground his teeth in a towering rage. Without gesture or further thought, he said, "Die." So they died at a word, and he reveled in the stench they left behind. There was nothing else left of them.

It is all clear now. I am Seer. Qiel had never abdicated in the first place. He had merely forgotten the truth. Red darkness filtered through the room. His horde grew thicker on the building, all converging on this place. He would begin his command here, where the earth was thinnest. From here, he could go in between realities at will. Even now, the room, the building, and the earth below flickered like a hot road in mid-summer.

CHAPTER XII

I WAS DEEP IN the belly of the beast. Once I finally landed on the bottom of its horrible-smelling stomach, I went to work. Riverso Tondo, a horizontal strike from left to right. The sword cut clean and without effort as I spun through a full 360 degrees, slicing the stomach in half.

Since the thing was so huge, I hadn't done much damage beyond, well, cutting the stomach in half. And then really pissing it off. It must have then twisted itself over because my world went berserk, pitching and rolling wildly.

I tried to get some footing or leverage inside, but the relative isolation of an intact stomach had given way to a flood of viscera and blood crowding in on me from all sides, and I couldn't breathe. I've had about enough of this. I crouched down and held the sword straight out. Giocco Stretto.

I summoned all my strength and then launched, Sword first, thinking of maximum speed and power. The force of my efforts not only sliced the beast through, but because of the blast of my light trail, also tore it asunder behind me.

Emerging into clean air upside down at—it took my eyes a

moment to calculate—9,800 feet.

The great demon stopped flapping its wings and groaned as it turned to ash. It rained down like black snow.

Hovering, soaked in blood and guts, the pure blue light that now resided in my heart glowed outward from me against a darkening sky. I huffed a lock of hair out of my face. Well, it's been worse, hasn't it?

I assessed the state of the battle. Straight below me was the tower. There was a new threat—the biggest demon I had ever seen.

Within the sweep of its wings, there were whole battalions of the enemy horde flying escort. It belched miles of scorching crystalline fire from its mouth, and wherever the clear flames licked, all life was desiccated.

This could only be the Devourer.

It was coming right at me. Still a few miles off, it released another burst of fire. The flames, which looked more like ripples of intense heat because they lacked all color, didn't quite reach me where I flew, but I could feel the sucking heat and I wasn't going to hang around until I got burned.

Taking off, I burst immediately to 500 miles per hour. Most of the guts came off me in the wind.

I looked behind me. With one sweep of its wings, the Devourer had halved the distance between us. Its mouth was opening.

I broke left, circling around the tower.

It followed instantly, loosing another barrage.

I dove for the ground and spun around, sword in the Guardia Seconda, angled up and to the left, the flat toward the blast so it could be deflected away from me.

It worked. I broke hard left again, buzzing around the tower like a fly being chased by a hungry bird.

The dragon gave chase, but it wasn't quite as agile as I was, nor as fast. I poured on the speed and circled around to attack it from behind.

It happened in the space of less than two seconds, but time slowed for me as I hacked my way through the lesser demons in the dragon's train. These were hangers-on, like pilot fish attending the shark, and they were quick work. Stocatta, Imbrocatta, Punta Riversi. And then Fendente as I brought the sword down along my own axis, hacking a devil in two from skull to pelvis.

I let fly my battle cry. It was like the shriek of an eagle. I was now chasing the Devourer—its tail was right over my head. I held the sword high and poured on more speed. The blade penetrated deep into its belly, cutting easily from the hindquarters to the ribs, its work like a heavenly rebuke. There was retribution interwoven in this blow, and I was reminded whose sword I wielded.

The beast reacted violently, moving into a displacement roll. With the tower to our left, it broke upward and to the right to get away from me. It barrel rolled, looped, and then banked back toward the tower in an effort to regain the advantage of pure pursuit.

But it was too late. Its wounds were too serious. Whatever its anatomical construction, something had come loose internally, and the fantastic heat and fire it was able to generate as its primary weapon now turned against it.

It caught fire, starting at the cut the sword had made in its gullet. Now completely out of control, it swooped numb and mostly dead directly toward the upper third of the tower.

CHAPTER XIII

MICHAEL WOKE WITH A killer headache.

But he was alone in an empty room, and when he looked around, he found that the door had been left open.

He knew his only chance was to run, to get out of there and hope Airel didn't come within a thousand miles of this area. His heart was that of a 12th round heavyweight fighter. All he wanted was to have a spare moment to cry for Ellie, to weep for the loss of Airel's father. There were fates worse than death, and being the Seer of the Brotherhood was at the top of that list.

Flexing his toes and fingers to be sure everything still worked, he struggled to his feet and crept to the door. He slipped into a painful run in the hallway. Through the tears that streamed down his face, he saw a bank of elevators. He pushed the DOWN button over and over again.

After a lifetime, the elevator "bong" went off. It was here.

The doors slid open too slowly. Still no one in the hallways. It was now or never. Michael practically leaped into the elevator and the beckoning safety of its capsule.

He pressed the button for the ground floor. It was time to get out of here. The excruciating second or two that elapsed in the interim between his floor selection and the eventual closing of the doors, he could hear the creature's growl rising in pitch and volume. It stood every hair of his body on end.

Somethings coming. The doors slid shut.

I COASTED TO A higher altitude as I watched the airborne remains of the Devourer collide with the tower. The explosion was immense, and it shook the structure to its core. Clear fire issued forth in fountains like water, erasing everything in its path, dissolving and blackening the things on which it landed like sulfuric acid, turning them to wrung-out charcoal.

The carcass had impacted the tower at its upper reaches, just below the spire. The collision split the creature in half along the cut I had made. The effect was akin to watching a stream pour around a stone deeply embedded in the ground. On the opposite side of the impact, there would be much destruction once the beast and the pieces of its unique chemical weapon finally touched down 150 stories below.

Higher up, where it had struck the building, I watched the spire sway under its own weight.

AS SOON AS THE doors closed, Michael felt everything explode. The building shook. The whole building, Michael thought. God help me.

Everything was very hot suddenly, and smoke was pouring downward through the gap in the doors. He had been thrown down onto the floor of the elevator, and he could feel it bounce on its cables. Now more than ever, he was acutely aware of the sheer height of his position. The meaning of the 150th floor was driven into his understanding like a 16d nail.

Then something dripped onto the floor of the elevator car, splattering and hissing. A drop flecked onto the skin of his forearm, and it stung bad. He swiped at it, making the pain worse. He looked up.

Something was dripping from the corner of the stainless-steel trim overhead. He made up his mind instantly that the elevator had outlived its usefulness. He resolved to get out of it.

He put his fingers in the seam between the doors and pulled. Something overhead groaned moving the elevator downward—he could see the floor of the lobby outside rise by a foot or more.

He pulled on the doors harder. He could now just barely fit through their width if he went one shoulder at a time.

More groaning—it sounded like the whole building was coming down around him. The lobby floor rose again, this time by three feet. His window of escape was now about twelve inches wide by twenty-four inches tall. He groaned one arm and shoulder out, his elbow cocked like a wing against the lobby floor, now at chest height, the fingers of his other hand hooked onto the piece of floor trim that, only a few seconds ago, he had walked right over as he'd gotten into this death trap.

The foremost fear in his mind was that he would get partway out only to be sliced in half by an elevator in sudden freefall. But there were worse ways to die. He knew that much from experience, especially lately.

He pushed off the floor and pulled himself upward and out, like getting out of a pool without a ladder.

He landed in the lobby, and just as he did, the elevator let go, taking one of his shoes with it. The tug of war hurt badly, and as he backed away from the edge it occurred to him that his ankle might now be sprained, if not broken.

He looked around in a panic. Was this the same place? Everything was different now, destroyed. The lights were out. Auxiliary lighting had come on, casting evil shadows. There were red letters on exit signs, emergency beacons were sounding off, and a few fire sprinklers above his head were spewing water. Everything was filthy—adding water to it just made thin mud. He leaned up against the opposite wall and tried to breathe, getting soaked.

Then it occurred to him: What is chasing me?

But he had an idea who or what it was. He didn't like his idea at all.

CHAPTER XIV

THE TOWER'S UPPERMOST VILLAGE. The tower's uppermost section was going to go. My eyes calculated the figures—the upper tip was in excess of 2,700 feet high, and where the dragon had collided wasn't more than 800 feet below that point. That would put the weak spot at the 150th floor, approximately.

That was where the structure was rotting through with phosphoric fire.

I circled around it, hacking my way through the cloud of demons the Devourer had left behind.

Far below, the demon's carcass finally impacted the ground. It had to have weighed in excess of 700 tons, about the takeoff weight of two lightly loaded Boeing 747s. This weight shook the earth, and as more acidic fire splashed down and out from the force of the impact, I couldn't help but smile.

The bigger they are . . .

THE WHOLE BUILDING SHOOK, prompting Qiel to walk over

to the windows. He knew what had happened already, but the vestiges of his humanity still wanted to chase ambulances. Glass and other debris rained down from high above. The lights flickered. Then there was the fire and flesh of the Devourer. Many would perish in the aftermath.

This is the fault of the halfbreed.

He would enjoy watching her writhe as the price was exacted from her. Even now Michael was running to "freedom"—perhaps that little piece of bait would turn the girl's head enough to give him the upper hand.

As for the forces he had sent to invade Eden, he could only assume their expedition had ended in failure. He would have to make do without the power of the Tree.

Sensing the hordes increasing weaknesses, Qiel drew the sea toward him and his legions. The sea would wipe the earth clean. The flood would burst forth and sweep away everything that was bigoted against him and his kind. El's angels would fall and decay in the quagmire.

Long tentacles lifted from the deep and lashed out, twisting and grasping, pulling down towers and bridges as the sea invaded the city and doused the fire of the Devourer. Qiel called upon his most powerful weapons now. The Seer would not lose the war to a little girl.

"Let's see what you think of this." He closed his eyes and imagined more, more.

THE SKY WAS BLACK now, and not totally because the sun had fled over the horizon. Floods of more Brotherhood poured from nowhere, appearing out of the air.

This is one of the thin places, like the Threshold in the house of Kreios.

Dragons from legends, serpents bearing wings, fanged monsters, insects as big as buses converged on the tower. There were beasts in the sky, beasts in the sea. The hope I'd had at the start—after I took out their two best and biggest—now faded. I couldn't even begin to count their numbers—my mind went numb at the sheer size of their army.

Circling around the tower, I looked out to the desert and saw only water. It moved as if alive and the tower stood amidst the sea like an upraised finger.

Something hit me broadside and I flew backward, tumbling out of control. I skipped across the water a few times like a flat stone. My head spinning, I rocketed into the air, gasping, trying to get my vision to clear.

A tentacle like a war monument took a swipe at me. I dodged just in time. The huge arm was made entirely of water, but that didn't mean it wasn't deadly. Okay, how do I kill a monster made only of water? Before I could figure that out, a swarm of demons converged upon me. I cut through them, feeling my exhaustion close in.

I'd been avoiding the obvious conclusion, and I was smarter than that. There was only one explanation for that with which I was now faced, but I avoided it because of what it would mean. Qiel must be the Seer now.

That meant Qiel had returned. From the dead? I didn't know. But the only angel I knew of who had this level of control over the sea was the son of Uriel. And if he was the Seer, that meant he was against us, despite his lineage. But more importantly, if Qiel was Seer, that meant Michael wasn't—he had failed. And if he had failed, that meant his life was in serious jeopardy. Come on, Kreios.

This would be a great time to show up.

Qiel controlled the sea—he had to have been behind the tsunami. Confirming my conclusions, even more tentacles rose up and wreaked havoc on the city of Dubai.

All I had to do was get to the Seer and kill him. That would end this war once and for all. Should be easy. Like slapping a mosquito. The size of Texas.

I gripped the sword tighter and was about to make a beeline for the top of the broken tower when I got snagged and wrapped up by a smaller tentacle. The Sword of Light vanished as I struggled. The monstrous arm grew in size and strength, feeding on the sea, dragging me from the sky and pulling me down into the waves, under the water.

I could hear laughing and curses. I held my breath, hoping for an opportunity to escape. My arms were pinned to my sides—the massive tentacle was crushing my ribcage. I had one last chance. I relaxed and let it all go, releasing my will in submission to El. The explosion of light that ripped from my heart ripped the tentacle to shreds. Thanks for that.

I launched toward the surface. When I broke free, coughing and gagging, I had to dodge more tentacles before I could fill my lungs with air. But I was snatched back by this forest of towering seas and dragged down again.

I sounded my battle cry under the waters.

Just then, the dark sky broke through with blazing light. Kreios appeared at the head of a terrible army of death, bathed in brilliant light. He scanned the battlefield, looking for something, someone.

Me.

CHAPTER XV

AS KREIS APPROACHED THE tower, he took off the head of the first demon he encountered with a single casual stroke. It gagged and fell, turning to a plume of ash before it hit the water.

He addressed the Armies of the Damned. "Murderers and host of the damned, clear a way to that tower." Kreios pointed with his sword to the Burj, the only building left standing. "I will find Airel. You will destroy every last beast of hell that moves. Leave none alive. You shall grant no mercy." If we're doing this, we're doing it all the way.

Kreios turned to Cain, who was at his side with his six. Only seven remained of the Eden Detachment. The Tree of Life was made safe; the Brotherhood invasion horde was wiped out. "You have fulfilled your promise so I fulfill mine." He swung his sword and killed Cain. Turning to the dead, he commanded, "Come, murderers and killers. Let us go see about provoking the end of the Brotherhood."

Then he heard the battle cry of his granddaughter. She had been dragged beneath the waves—she needed help. He shot toward her, leaving a trail of light and ash behind him. He could hear his armies behind him cutting through demon flesh, which made him smile. It was a good sound, a holy sound.

Death became him. Going before and behind the angel Kreios was a vanguard of withering eradication. His presence now tunneled through, cast aside, and utterly ruined everything it touched.

Including the sea.

The towers of grasping water gave way around him and the pale light that surrounded his person. The sea gave up the girl, and he took her up into his arms and flew high above the battle, out of the reach of the writhing watery shapes.

He let her go. She was soaked to the bone. "Are you okay?" he asked.

Airel ran a hand through her wet hair and nodded, breathing deep. "You came. I needed you, and you came."

Kreios took her in his arms and hugged her tight. "I love you, Airel. Of course I came."

They drew apart, and she looked at herself. "At least I'm not covered in demon innards anymore."

"Airel," Kreios pointed downward, "do you know why the sea has grown arms?" Kreios had never seen such a thing under the sun.

"I think it's Qiel. I think he's the Seer."

"Who is Qiel?"

"We don't have time, and I'm pretty sure Michael's is running out too. Do you know where he is? Can you sense him?"

"Do not lose hope, Airel—all is not lost. Michael is there." He pointed to the tower far below them. "If we finish well, we can make him safe."

In dramatic fashion, the Sword of Light returned to her hand. The sight of his granddaughter wielding the weapon he himself had used in the dispatch of so many demon Brothers sent a chill of pride through him every time.

Airel cricked her neck and stretched.

Kreios could feel the drain cease with the advent of the Sword. Airel touched his hand. "Ready?"

Kreios narrowed his eyes. "Ready."

QIEL REMAINED, ROBED IN white silk, at the wall of windows, surveying his domain. Right at eye level there were two angels, pure and light, and dare he even think the word holy, terrible to behold, wrestling in midair with a crimson-skinned devil. As the three figures grappled, the demon flapped like a struggling bat, coming closer to the floor-to-ceiling windows where Qiel stood. One of the angels gave the whole tangle a hard shove and they all three crashed into the thick glass, shaking the wall.

Qiel saw up close the look of determination on the face of one of the angels. There was sweat and struggle there, just on the other side of the glass. He could hear the muted sounds of the contest, heard the monosyllabic ejaculations that were standard issue in combat. He also heard words spoken in a language he didn't know, but nevertheless he recognized.

That disturbed him.

It was the language the angels were speaking.

One of them drew a dagger, which shone brightly even in this darkness. Still pinning the crimson-skinned bat against the glass, the dagger-wielding angel gave a shout and then plunged it into the demon's torso. The struggle slowly diminished, and in the background, other details became clear to Qiel. Angels streaking on trails of pure white light and what looked to be the damned—two or three to a demon—chasing them down and abusing, even bullying them into submission. They came from above and below; they were everywhere.

But finally his eyes were drawn to the scene directly in front of him. The crimson bat's wings fell limp. The angel withdrew his dagger, and then the two members of the angelic army released their victim. The bat's sweat and blood streaked the glass as gravity took it down.

He stepped closer to the glass and peered downward to see the demon fall. Its wings fluttered rippling against the uprush. It didn't reach the ground. It crashed onto the roof of one of the lower sections, still a hundred stories up. A scavenger demon came instantly to feed upon its corpse.

Farther down, the cost of the battle was laid out before him in furious display, a shameless kind of candor. The sea ran red.

He raised his gaze and saw them—Airel and Kreios, together, tearing through his horde as if the Brothers were but powerless children. Airel was unmistakable, wielding the Sword of Light and bathed in hateful blue. Kreios was death itself, mounted upon the spectre of a great pale horse that sped across the skies, taking souls to Abaddon unimpeded.

Qiel clenched his fists, bringing forth the sea and all his creatures, attacking on every front. But it was in vain—the dead were unaffected, even untouched by the peak of his powers. The enemy's armies were not of this world. How to go about killing something that's already dead? Despite all the Bloodstone had given him, despite all it knew and all the wonders it held, there was no incantation, no magic for this. Kreios and Airel glided through his wielded waters as if he was nothing.

Cursing, the Seer turned away from the scene. His demon Brothers were falling much too fast; the men didn't even enter into the equation. The drain, so reliable, so potent in the past, was now also not a factor. The Sword Airel held protected them.

She is the key.

If he didn't kill her, this long-awaited war would be lost in a matter of moments.

It is time for a change in strategy.

CHAPTER XVI

MICHAEL WAS IN GREAT pain. It wasn't just his ankle. He wore his grief like a cloak of many sorrows now, and it was very heavy. He had failed to procure the Bloodstone, failed to destroy it. He had failed to protect anyone—Uriel was dead. John was worse. Michael knew Airel was out there somewhere, that she would risk everything to try to get to him and bust him out of captivity, so that made him a liability. What kind of hero needs to be rescued by the princess? He had failed at everything; he couldn't even ride an elevator properly. Now simply escaping with his life seemed impossible.

Through the darkness, through mists thrown down by the handful of fire sprinklers that were subduing the dust and cinders in the air, he could see a black lump on the ground. A dead man? He looked to be dead; one leg splayed awkwardly to the side. Where is his demon Brother?

The building shook again. It was like being in the bowels of a ship on a weather-beaten sea, tossed like a toy, and there were no windows here in the elevator lobby of the 150th floor. There was no point of reference—only this sickening motion.

More groaning from overhead. Ripping, tearing. Crumbling.

Something was coming down the elevator shaft, coming for him fast. He needed to get out now. But his ankle handicapped him. He hobbled away from the elevators as fast as he could.

He eyed the dark lump as he passed, wondering if the man was really dead.

Then the blackened pile stirred.

Michael felt fear again. He was still in grave danger—he needed to find something with which to arm himself, and quick.

"Why . . . if it isn't . . . the Alexander," the man said, his voice a gurgle. "The luckiest man on the face of the earth." He choked and struggled to breathe, but with his one remaining arm, he finally managed to draw and level a pistol at his target.

"I guess El takes care of His own," Michael said. "How's your career choice working out for you?"

The man took a shot and it went wide and high, impacting the wall somewhere behind him. He was in the last stages of severe shock, his arm shaking violently and his breaths shallow and rapid. He squeezed the trigger again.

This shot grazed Michael's left arm, causing a flash of pain. But as he grabbed at the wound, he could see that the pistol's slide had locked open—out of ammo. "Hmm. I guess I am pretty lucky."

"Die!" the man screamed, yanking the trigger, furious, his epithet drawn out loud and long.

"Soon enough," he said.

A wicked smile then came over the man's face as he said, "Soon . . . there." He degraded into spits and coughs.

Michael turned to see the man's Brother approaching from behind. It was the better part of half a demon, missing one arm and a wing, and it had suffered a crippling wound in one of its legs. It limped closer, hauling itself along the filthy travertine, hissing foul obscenities and threats.

Michael stepped to the man and kicked him in the head, putting him out of his misery. He grabbed the pistol from his hand and threw it as hard as he could at the demon. It bounced off it's thick forehead, stunning it for a moment. It crouched and roared at him. Michael had reached his breaking point. He roared back. "Hey, stupid," he said, opening his arms wide. "Why don't you just eat me?"

But the demon slowed, collapsing to the floor. He thought it had died, but it was looking past him toward the elevator lobby. Michael spun around and saw a fresh one clawing its way through the elevator doors. Lights flickered overhead and Michael stood with most his weight on his good leg. "Oh, come on. When will this stop?"

The demon threw the doors back with violence and they stuck, jammed and askew. It emerged into the hallway crouched, wings tucked behind it, at least seven feet tall and completely uninjured.

Michael had no weapon, so he decided to try a different tactic. "Listen to me, demon: I am the rightful Seer. I command you to bring me the Bloodstone and kill the traitor who holds it."

The demon slowed its advance, evidently considering things. Another one climbed out of the shaft and spoke in a low hiss. "You were the chosen one, the Alexander; next in the line Tengu created. By right, the throne was yours. But we can serve only the one who holds the stone. And now you are only bait."

"I demand to speak to the prince."

A croak vibrated through both their bellies, but Michael stood his ground, hoping they did not sense his fear.

"Impossible. The prince is not one to obey demands, nor would he hold court with a boy."

Michael took two steps toward them and raised his voice. "I am no boy. I am your Seer, Bloodstone or no."

Blankness and silence. Then, "Or we could kill you and be on our way."

Michael scoured the hall for anything he could use as a weapon. There. Under the dead man. He rolled the corpse aside and took the nightstick from his belt. "If you want a fight, you got one."

Yet they held. There was no attack.

Michael sensed with growing alarm the truth—he was being held here for a reason.

He did the only thing he could do. He turned and ran away as fast as his limp would allow.

THE SKY BLAZED WHITE as the host of heaven descended.

Kreios finally allowed himself a respite and cast his eyes to the heavens. Descending toward him were the kinsmen he knew and loved so well. Yamanu. Zedkiel. Veridon. Called back and fully restored to grace and power in this, their finest hour. To have Airel at his side in witness of these glorious events was indeed gratifying.

She bore the Sword of Light, El's own Sword. Cloud and light passed through the perfectly strange opening at its hilt. Kreios added it to the clutch of mysteries coming forth on this day, a day when he saw a great many things he never would have dared to imagine.

The Brotherhood was yet to be routed. They were beaten back, but not beaten, and the Seer still obviously held his ground in the tower. But as Kreios flew through these striated skies with the remnant of the two-thirds at his side, he sensed a fundamental shift in the battle.

They will now flee to the far corners of the earth. "We must ensure that none of them live! We must deliver to them the price of their rebellion!" The angels of El had suffered many losses at the hands of the Brotherhood enemy over the centuries, but they had always outnumbered them two to one, at least in total. Now their full angelic number had assembled, and the day of vengeance had finally arrived.

"Go and get them," he said, and the host of El flew, followed by the dead, set to fight one last time.

THE WATER MONSTER THAT had tangled itself around the tower was the biggest danger to us—it was demolishing any angelic force that was out of range of the Sword's protection. The Seer was somewhere in the tower, and I needed to see for myself if things had developed as I feared. Michael, my Michael, could be in grave danger. He could be in need of rescue.

Help me be strong, keep my heart open, and show me what I should do.

Kreios cut a wing off a nearby demon and shoved the creature toward me. I ran it through, turning it to ash. He gave me a slight nod and we saw the army of the damned coming around the north side of the tower. The Brotherhood horde would fall—victory would be ours.

I sounded my eagle battle cry, and a shout rippled through the heavenly host. The attack ordered, the angels rallied in pursuit of the enemy.

I raised my blade and looked at Kreios, nodding toward the tower. "Time for us to meet the new Seer. You with me?"

Kreios smiled. The Sword cleared a path for us.

CHAPTER XVII

AS WE NEARED THE TOWER, I felt the Sword gain incremental power. It began to buzz, sending a tingle up my arm. We poured on the speed.

Kreios hacked and batted demons away like flies. I didn't have to do much anymore; the Sword was taking center stage now. The round space in the hilt glowed around its circumference as if the metal were in a forge; it looked white hot, but it was cool to the touch. Demons began to cower at our approach. Some covered their ears or eyes as if in pain, and their flight paths grew erratic as they fell away.

We were now closer than we'd ever been to the epicenter of the battle, to the place where the Seer and the power of the Bloodstone dwelled. Qiel had drawn up columns of water over most of the tower's exterior. Some were buttresses of ice. The darkness here was thick. But the light that poured from the Sword and radiated from my heart was all the brighter for it.

I watched the state of those parts of the battle that were up close to the tower. Qiel was very powerful—wherever an angel flew, bits of ice would explode outward from the tower, blasting saltwater shrapnel at El's army. Some of the blasts were so indiscriminate as to also take out the Seer's own Brotherhood forces. It was a stupid, desperate way to fight. I sensed the end drawing near.

It was a singular spectacle, like being a battlefield observer of a conflict in which the combatants were not clearly declared by their color of uniform, their aspect, or some other feature. The armies of the damned, allied with El? Killers, joining in the fight against the forces of darkness? It was difficult for me to believe my eyes. All I could do was trust and carry on.

Kreios and I looped around the tower, close enough to feel the constant danger posed by the power of the Seer and his Bloodstone, close enough to feel the Sword wrestling the darkness away. Close enough to feel our vulnerability.

"Airel, dive!" Kreios shouted, alerting me to a blast of ice. I reacted quickly, avoiding most of it by the breadth of a hair. Some smaller pieces raked me, and as the seawater melted into my wounds, it stung and ached. I recovered quickly and gained altitude. Closer. Faster. Let's end it now.

My strategy was simply to bring the blade closer to the Seer. It was a contest of proximity—two things could not dwell in the same space. I would force the issue. We shall see who prevails—the Creator or the created.

I felt the very air tremble as I drew near to the Seer's seat of power.

The skies overhead were beginning to thin and clear out. Most of the Brotherhood force had fled, having been scattered by El's armies. I could see the sun, just barely peeking from behind the clouds. The water below was not raging as it had before, and some dry spots were beginning to appear. It's working. All I had to do was bring the sword to bear. The enemy was beginning to flee.

But then the tower began to shake. Slabs of ice weighing many tons broke off and began to fall. The whole building then erupted in angry violence, and masses of ice and glass went into freefall. When the explosion went off, sending a shockwave through the atmosphere for miles around, I knew it was all over.

We had won.

WE LIT NEAR THE top of the wreckage, 150 floors up. This was the Brotherhood command post; there was no doubting the smell. Kreios and I were both in the guard, blades raised and ready as we searched the shell of the top of the tower. The spire had broken off in the conflict.

We split up in our search for the enemy.

Soon it became obvious. The Seer was gone.

Reports came to our minds from miles away, from Yamanu and Zedkiel and Veridon—the Brotherhood was no more. All had been vanquished. The Bloodstone? The Seer? None of us were sure, but I could not feel either anymore.

I relaxed for the first time, feeling every tired and sore muscle. My bones hurt. "Kreios?" Silence.

I glanced out over the lost city of Dubai through the twisted remains of the structure as I picked my way through the rooms.

I found Kreios crouched over remains, whether human or angelic, I couldn't be sure. I approached. Blood covered the floor at his knees, and his shoulders heaved in great, quiet sobs of grief. It was the body of a woman—from the awkward curve of her neck, I could see that it had been broken. Her face was mostly eaten away. Her hair was electric blue.

I ran to Kreios.

He held Ellie's ruined body in his arms, her poor, awful head in his lap. I couldn't breathe. My legs buckled and I fell next to him. We wept together.

Kreios roared. It was loud and long, and it hinted of a story filled to overflowing with frustration and pain and longing.

My mind was numb, beneath reason. I felt all my hope vanish. The war, the Seer—none of it mattered anymore. Why did Ellie have to die? My eyes were clamped tight shut and Kreios didn't try to comfort me. I hadn't the strength anymore to comfort him.

We were lost in our own grief.

But then I sensed Michael for the first time in forever, not far off. I could hear him. He needed me. I was on my feet in an instant, and running.

MICHAEL HAD RUN OUT of luck, run out of rooms.

They had chased him into an office with a single door. There was a wall of windows to his right, a door guarded by two demons to his left, and nowhere to go. There was no way out. His back to the wall, he faced down his demons, nothing but a stupid club in his hand, a night watchman's trinket. "I'm not dying without a fight." He prepared for the worst.

"Michael!" It was a desperate, feminine, beautiful sound. It was Airel.

At the sound of her voice, the two pursuing demons froze.

"Airel." He lowered his club as the demons turned away from him to investigate this new development. "You showed up just in time."

Airel stood bold as a warrior woman, covered in blood and sweat. Her shirt clung to her, torn and dirty, but light emanated from the pure place of her one and only heart, scars and all. She was the most beautiful thing he had ever seen.

"Hey. You two." She puffed her hair out of her face. "You do know you're the last two, right? Do you really want to mess with me?" The Sword of Light appeared from out of elsewhere into her left hand, its blade bathed in white fire, and she casually held it there.

The demons squirmed and tripped over each other trying to back up. "Who is this?" one of them hissed.

"I am Airel, daughter of El."

They cowered and whimpered like frightened dogs, looking for a way out.

She pointed. "And that is my boyfriend. And I am going to kill you. Now."

They made a dash for the windows.

She gave chase.

Before they could make it through, they were dead. As the momentum of her strike carried them onward, they shattered the glass with their corpses, already beginning to turn to ash. Airel finished with a flourish, crouching low in a skid at the building's edge, blade swept across and down to one side, head bowed in reverential control. The demons descended in an arcing plume toward the earth below.

Michael took a deep breath and dropped his weapon, sinking to the floor, back still to the wall. "That was pretty hot, babe."

The sword vanished from sight. Airel came to him and wrapped her arms around his neck, kissing him fiercely. "Michael, I'm so glad you're not dead."

He pulled her closer and they kissed, but they drew apart and just breathed the air of the aftermath. It was finally over.

He noticed now for the first time that he felt much better. The Bloodstone had to be gone for good, and he would be left alone now that it had a new host.

He pulled her face closer, his fingers tangled in her lovely long dark hair, his hand moving up her neck to the curve of the back of her head, buried deep there in those intimate places. He kissed her lips in painfully gentle love, savoring all of her nearness, feeling in his heart at last a consummation and release now that they could finally be together. "I love you," he breathed.

She seemed to drink him in with her eyes. "I love you too, Michael."

Their words were few.

CHAPTER XVIII

BACK HOME. THOSE TWO words were filled with equal amounts of hope and pain. So much had been lost, so many things would never be the same ever again. And yet this place in the mountains, in the midst of an anomaly where time didn't mean the same thing as it did in the rest of the world, was as much home as home could be under the sun.

It's a good place to camp out. That's how I felt. Having seen the things I'd seen, having done the things I'd done . . . well, I just couldn't give the real world much weight anymore.

This was where I'd found my one and only love, suffered real betrayal, suffered death, lived again, trained my hands for war, and came to know my grandfather, an angel of El. If home was where the heart was, home was right here. The people I loved were here. Those who were not here lived on in fond memory.

Hope and pain.

Hope and pain, a marriage of opposites. That's what life under the sun was—tension.

It had been months since Dubai. The world was a wreck, and it would never be the same. The changes wrought by the war were too profound to begin to catalogue, but I resolved to keep a journal about as much of it as I could manage. In essence, things were much quieter, and that was both good—hopeful—and bad because the world overflowed with the pain of its losses. And it still struggled with the disbelief of what it had seen.

After the war, El recalled the two-thirds. The host of heaven crossed over to elsewhere, paradise, rising upward beyond where the thin places could touch. Before going, the war captains reported success on all fronts, though there were two loose ends—the Seer and the Bloodstone. Those kills had never been confirmed. Kreios and I could only assume the worst then. My biggest clue that things were unfinished was that I could still call up the Sword of Light at will. I trained with it daily early mornings in Kreios's dojo.

Home.

Yet I still felt unsettled, as if I was the one thing on earth that didn't belong here. I couldn't shake the feeling that even though I'd learned to let go—to give in to the link between my true identity and the will of El—something was still out of order. Something was still wrong. I guess that's how we know there's still work to be done.

I was completely lost as to my dad, and I craved closure. I brought him up with Michael once, but things became so awkward between us, I let it go. I could only assume he hadn't made it through the war. And I couldn't ask Kreios because after he left to bury Ellie, he hadn't come home. Like so many things in life, I would have to content myself to wait for the answers.

Michael's ankle had healed to the point that he could walk on it again, though he told me it still bothered him when the weather was changing. "You're just getting old," I told him, which provoked a love punch in the shoulder. Oh, how I loved that man. I was convinced there was no greater joy than to be in love with your best friend in the whole wide world.

One morning after breakfast, we decided to put his bum ankle to the test and walk out to the cliffs. We hadn't been there since . . . well, since a lifetime ago. Michael and I descended the long stairway to the meadow, holding hands and watching an eagle soar high in the cool autumnal blue-eyed bliss above us. "Your ankle okay?" I asked.

"Yeah," he said.

"Good. I'm glad." I bumped into him as we walked, rubbing our arms together, and he smiled at me.

"Do you think Kreios will find anything this time?"

"Heck if I know," I said. "Do I look like a Seer to you? I can't predict the future."

He sighed. "I sometimes wish none of this ever happened. Except you, of course."

"I guess that's the price we pay for being perfect for each other." I was feeling a little silly.

"We've both been through a lot; it changes you. I don't see how we could come out of this stuff unchanged."

"Change for the better, though, in the end. Right?"

He put his arm around me. "Right."

He still could make me crazy with a look or a simple touch. Was he perfect? Not by a long shot. But who was I to talk?

We came to the woods that separated the meadow from the cliffs. "Airel, do you ever dream of anything anymore? Sometimes I dream of the day we can go for a walk, hold hands—"

"Um," I held up our interlocked hands, "what are we doing right now, then? Going for a drive?"

"And come home to our house. And go to sleep and wake up next to each other."

My heart began to race. He could do that to me with such ease.

"You know, we could be two old people, doing crosswords on the back porch, watching the sunset, drinking iced tea."

"Coffee for me, pal. I'm not a tea girl."

"Yeah, well, we'll be old, so it had better be decaf, right? We don't want you to trip and break your hip getting to the bathroom at three a.m."

"Jeez, Michael, that's so sweet that you want our life together to grow into this perfect cliché," I teased him.

He chuckled. It was a nice sound, one I hadn't heard much lately and one I hoped to hear more of in the days to come.

"Do you think it will ever be like that for us?" I lifted my face to the golden rays of the sun as they filtered through the red-orange-yellow leaves of the forest. We had talked like this before, of course. But part of me wondered what was going on inside that sensitive and brilliant head of his.

Michael sighed. "I don't know. Maybe not . . ."

"Maybe not? What?" I pivoted on a hair trigger and got short with him.

"Airel, hang on. This isn't one of those 'if we were the last two people on earth' kinds of scenarios. You and I chose each other."

"We sure did."

"I'm just saying we have a lot to work out between us. I mean . . ."

"Yes?"

"I'm just saying . . . Have you thought about the age thing?"

"Michael, what are you trying to say?" But I knew.

"You'll be young forever—"

I cut him off. "I do age. Just very slowly."

"Yeah. Slowly." He stopped and reached out to hold my chin with a finger and I let him, drinking him in. He took a moment to put his words together carefully—I could see it in his eyes. "Airel, will you still love me when I'm an old man?"

My brows furrowed. "Of course," I breathed, but my heart blanched at the cold way he posed the question.

"This is our reality, Airel. I mean, will we ever have children? Should we?"

I turned aside and walked off the path. "I don't want to talk about this. Can't we just pretend everything's going to be okay, Michael?" I gazed at the filtered sun. Leaves flitted high above. I watched one fall.

"Is that what you really want, Airel? The fairy tale? The dream?"

"No. Yes." I rubbed my face in frustration.

"Because when you grow up, you come to find out the fairy tale is a lie. I'm surprised you don't know that yet."

I turned and stuck my finger in his chest. "Oh, I know it, Michael. I know all about it. I wear the scar on my heart that proves it, buddy." I opened the collar of my shirt. "Your own father gave me this wound, Michael, and not very far from here."

That hurt him. "Airel, I . . . that's not what I was trying to say . . . trying to do here." Finally he said, "I'm sorry."

"I'm sorry too, Michael."

With tears in his eyes, he pressed his fingers to his abdomen. "I have my own wound too, Airel."

And I remembered how it had all unfolded that day, how he didn't hesitate to do whatever it took to save me. I reached out and touched the hand that touched his wound. "We both have scars."

He held me tight on the trail for a long time, and we cried. "What a beautiful disaster we are, huh?" he said, pulling away and wiping his eyes. "Oh, God." He shook his head. "How come I can never quite do what I really want to do with you? You make me so crazy."

I laughed through my tears. "Ditto."

"I just want to know it will be fine—more than fine."

"You're looking for guarantees?"

He shoved his hands in his pockets and turned away.

"Because guarantees are for fairy tales," I continued. "Kid stuff." I waved my arms dramatically. "Things smart people like us have learned to do without."

He still faced away from me. "I fell for you the moment I first laid eyes on you, Airel. I didn't know who you were, but when we ran into each other in that coffee shop, I knew. I knew. I chose you right there and then." He turned back toward me.

I caught my breath looking into his eyes.

"All I know is that I'm lost without you. I know it will be hard, but I swear I will fight for you, pursue your love every day of my life. I'll never give up, I'll always be there for you—until the day I die. Old man or not."

He was holding something in his hands. They were cupped together, as if holding a drink of cool water. There on the trail in the woods dappled by autumn sunlight, he got on one knee. He winced a little as his bum ankle flexed, but he managed. When my eyes focused, I could see that he was holding a ring.

"Airel, will you marry me?"

It was a ring I knew well. It had belonged to my mom.

CHAPTER XIX

HE SLIPPED THE RING on my finger. It was made of pure silver and bore a single silvery blue pearl center mounted with tiny diamonds all around its base. It was like a flower opened with this blue pearl revealed inside it.

"Michael." I was gasping for breath.

He was still on one knee. I knew my answer, but I couldn't give it. I was tongue-tied.

I didn't need to see the change that crawled up over his face like a death masque to know the bottom had just dropped out of our world, and at the worst possible moment. The sword came to my hand without me even thinking of it, asking for it, or wanting it.

Michael's eyes were large and dark as he looked behind me at what was coming for us. "Oh, my God, Airel. I thought I would have time to be able to figure out a way to tell you."

"Tell me what?" I turned around.

"But there's no more time," Michael said from behind me. I could hear him struggle to his feet.

There before me, not ten feet away, was my dad. "Hello, Airel."

"Dad?"

He smirked. "Qiel." He took a breath, and in the most casual of tones, said, "You have been a bad girl, running away, not telling me that you were, well . . . not human." It was as if he was sighing over a broken cup.

"Qiel?" It can't be. Qiel was the son of Uriel.

"It is my fault, really. I should never have fathered you, never married your mother, and I should have killed you in your crib."

The Bloodstone hung from his neck like a bloody orb. This was Qiel, whom I had suspected was the Seer in Dubai—which, it turned out, I had been right about. I hated being right sometimes. And I hated myself for not figuring out this riddle. Of course. It's the only thing that makes any sense. I knew Qiel was in my lineage, but I didn't know he was my father.

"Ah, look how the hideous light of comprehension dawns upon her." With his right hand, Qiel drew a black dagger. "Fear not. I come to right my wrongs. I come to repair the damages." He took a swipe at me.

The sword, either on its own or connected by training to my instincts, moved to block the blow. The blades rang out in steel tones through the forest as we jostled for position on the path.

Michael tried to come around from behind me, but I kept him at my back, me and the sword between him and this new threat.

My mind was racing to keep up with the context of what was happening. I prayed to El I could remain detached and martial, calculating and sharp. I fought hard against my emotions to keep them in check.

"Do you wonder how this happened, halfbreed? Do you wonder if you can reach me? Save me from myself?"

No, no, no, don't give in to this! Keep your emotions in check.

"I can assure you, girl, you are the one who needs saving, not me."

"No." I said. I won't fight you. I spun around and launched myself at Michael, striking him with my shoulder firmly at his midsection. He was stunned and complained a little, but I didn't care. I held him over my shoulder in a fireman's carry as I gained altitude and flew up through the trees, taking to the skies. I would make him safe.

A burst of red exploded around us, sapping my power, and I faltered. "Oh, no." We were falling.

"Airel?" Michael said, his voice sounding alarmed. "Can you please do something? We're falling."

"I know, Michael!" I rolled us over, placing him on top of me as we descended. It happened fast. We plowed through the tips of the trees and crash-landed together on my back, coming to a stop near the cluster of boulders at the top of the cliff.

Qiel was coming. I could feel it. All those years. All that time you spent away. Holidays gone, Christmases spent without you. No wonder now. No wonder. Business trips and excuses and hidden love. I was beyond hurt.

"Michael, are you okay?"

He groaned. "Yeah."

"Then can you please get off me? I have the Seer to kill." Michael rolled off onto the ground, and as I clambered to my feet, I found myself in a wicked déjà vu. What is it about this cliff top and death? It was an evil place.

Qiel appeared at the edge of the forest. He advanced toward me. "Come, come, child. You must face the truth. You are an abomination, a curse. You should not exist."

"No," I said. "I am no mistake. I am a daughter of El."

"No," he said, "you are a disease. You are the key, Airel—don't you understand? You are the essence of the audacity of El. When I finally snuff out your life, the world will be made right, and truth and justice will prevail. The rebellion will finally be justified."

"Your truth and justice are lies," I said. "Your mind has been poisoned." I had lost track of Michael, but I didn't have time to wonder. He had climbed up to the top of one of the boulders unseen, and now, before I could stop him, he leaped for the Seer.

Qiel caught him by the throat and held him off the ground. "Stupid boy. I never did like you much."

"Let him go," I said, pointing the sword at my father. "Or I will kill you." But I wasn't close enough to follow through on my threat.

"Kill me if you can," he said, shrugging. He stabbed his black dagger deep into Michael's chest and then dropped him to the ground in a heap.

CHAPTER XX

"NO!" I SCREAMED.

Michael lay on the ground, gasping and wide-eyed.

My heart was ripped in half. I wanted to run to him, but I had to keep a wary eye on the Seer. I stood halfway between them, not knowing what to do.

Qiel's hand gestured toward my Michael. I could do nothing but stand by and watch helplessly as he manipulated the blood that spilled from Michael's chest. He drew it out into the air, gathered it together, and then forced it back in through the wound, where the effects were all too terrifying and obvious—he was flooding his lungs with blood, and Michael was drowning.

"No!" I pleaded. "Stop, please!"

My father smirked. "Witness the servant of El begging like a dog. This pleases me."

I fell to my knees and wailed, the sound coming out like the miserable screech of a wounded eagle. It was like the inverse of my battle cry. It was the desperate cry of a daughter for a hero.

"THE STONE WAS STOLEN from paradise when the Sons of El fell . . . a pure union of diamond and onyx . . . it glows red on earth in the presence of the spirit of the Seer . . . it does not belong here in the earthly realm."

These truths came to Kreios as he flew low over the meadow at high speed, his contrail burning a path in the grasses below. He wondered why El would quicken his heart to these specific legends about the Bloodstone, but there was no mistaking the cry of his granddaughter. It was a sound he had come to know and love, and now it was more desperate than he had ever heard it.

I am coming, daughter. I am coming.

The forest ripped apart as he tore through it.

As he broke free of the trees, he saw the Seer, his back to his approach, crouched low with hand outstretched toward Michael. He was killing him. Kreios bristled in anger, opening his arms wide to catch his prey.

IN A FLASH, KREIOS burst from the woods, tackling Qiel in midair. One instant he was there, the next, there was only dust, and Michael and I were alone. I dropped the sword. It clanged to the ground, bounced, and disappeared. I ran to Michael's side and skidded to my knees.

I held his head in my hands. "Michael, no. Don't go."

He was struggling. His eyes were wide and glassy and he wasn't breathing, but he saw me. He pulled my hands away from his face, grasping my left and squeezing the ring he had placed on my finger. Our eyes met.

His intentions were clear. His unspoken last words were without doubt that he loved me. The ring proved it.

This, his last act now done, I could see total rest enter his eyes. He was at peace. The one I loved, my one and only was gone, forever.

KREIOS CARRIED HIS LOAD over the cliff's edge and dropped it to the lake below. The drain was very strong—he could not hold on for long.

He looped skyward and circled back around toward Airel and Michael.

He checked back over his shoulder toward the Seer, looking for the moment of impact on the lake's surface, but that didn't happen. The surface was instead like glass. The Seer had disappeared.

I WAS STILL IN shock when Kreios landed at my side. He opened his arms to me and I fell into them, trying to breathe. I didn't have the strength to explain anything that had happened in the last two minutes. I opened my mind to him and let the reel of my memories roll. That was how the story would be told. Without words.

KREIOS FOUND SADNESS RUNNING through his body like a torrent. Qiel, son of Uriel, is the Seer? Airel, daughter of Qiel, is the key? His granddaughter was now betrothed to the dead? It was too much even for him, and he wondered at the meaning of it all. The sword is gone too? What shall we do?

Kreios let Airel go. She stood behind him as he stepped to the edge of the cliff and searched down into the deep water below, out across the lake. He considered this—in order to defeat the Seer, he would have to kill his daughter's only son. He grunted and narrowed his eyes. He knew how often El answered the why question: never. Not on this side, anyway. But he still wanted to ask it.

But there wasn't time for philosophy. The Sword of Light, the warmaker, had returned to his hand. He turned back toward Airel, ready to ask her what she thought this meant, when he saw Qiel rising from the earth behind her like water bubbles from a silent spring. "Airel! Behind you!"

I WATCHED IN DISBELIEF as my grandfather turned toward me, the sword in his hand.

"Airel! Behind you!" Kreios called out, reaching for me.

I spun, but it was too late. Something stabbed me in the back. It hurt more than anything I'd ever felt. I looked down to see the point of his dagger twisting up and out from my chest.

I completed my turn, breathless, and beheld my father and the smug triumph on his face, the cup of his betrayal now filled to the brim.

She rustled within me one last time. "Your time is short. What is your final move?"

I honestly didn't know. But as I stood there, stunned, my vision turning red, I saw a nightmare of which I could not be afraid anymore because it could not touch me: A red sea rising, a voice telling me, "You are the key, Airel."

And then I knew. It was so simple. And now, it was easy. Qiel thought he had won.

But he hadn't. In fact, he had only ever played into El's hand.

My final act was calm, still, and elegant, and I knew it would mean everything. I reached out to the Bloodstone that hung from his neck and, with the brush of a finger, I touched it.

After that, I was gone. I never even felt my body hit the ground.

KREIOS COULDN'T GET TO Airel in time. He was forced to watch her body crumple, lifeless, to the ground. But he had felt the whole world change when she touched the Bloodstone.

The words poured back into him:

The stone was stolen from paradise when the Sons of El fell . . . a pure union of diamond and onyx . . . it glows red on earth in the presence of the spirit of the Seer . . . it does not belong here in the earthly realm.

The look on the Seer's face said it all—the war was over, and he had lost.

At last, Kreios thought.

They both watched as the Bloodstone lifted free of its chain, lifted free of his influence, of the bond of blood, of the conduits to the prince.

Kreios hovered, the warmaker Sword of Light in his hand once more, and the stone was borne aloft with him.

The redness poured from the stone in a sea of blood, draining from it all darkness, all iniquity, all bloodshed, and the red ran into the ground at the cliff's edge. Kreios looked on as the stone became pure, as Qiel found himself welded to the earth from whence he had come. From where he had risen to the fulfillment of his masterful plot, he was now stuck like a weed to the spot of the betrayal of his only daughter.

The stone hovered directly over him, and he began to drown in the blood to which his life had been bound.

And then the ultimate came to pass—the marriage of the stone to the Sword of Light. Both were borne aloft and Kreios hovered higher, looking on as the stone became brilliant, dazzling white, light pouring from its every facet, coming nearer, fitting perfectly into the opening in the hilt.

It was as if it had been made that way from the Beginning.

CHAPTER XXI

KREIOS KNEW NOTHING WOULD bring Airel back. There would be no writing in a book, no more misplaced hopes.

He was alone again.

Losing Airel caused him to remember how painful it could be to love. It had been a long time, but love was still worth what it cost.

Everything, sometimes.

The Seer was vanquished. He had been Stanley Alexander, he had been Airel's father. He was nothing but dust.

Kreios would stand guard now until the End. As he hovered high above the clouds, above the domain with which he was charged, he looked at the sword he now held once again, and finally.

The jewel adorning its hilt was beautiful and spectacular. It seemed like it was partial, if a stone could be such a thing, to the same colors of blue he used to love seeing so much . . . streaking across the skies, full of power and life and fury.

Like an eagle.

THIS WAS NOT THE Kreios I knew.

He held in his hand a scythe. He was robed in pale darkness.

He held a hand out to me. "It is time, my daughter. You have done well. Do not be afraid."

I wasn't. All my fear was gone. I was ready. It was time for me to go home.

I WALKED IN A high meadow in the mountains.

It might have been the meadow near to the house of Kreios. It might not have been.

There was a path in the shape of a ring, and I saw high flowers dancing amongst green grasses in the most vibrant colors I'd ever beheld.

I felt light enough to fly without even trying.

As I walked along, I could tell I wasn't alone. There was within my heart what others might have called anticipation, excitement— but using these words would be like painting with blacks and whites when the landscape was in fact sacred blue, verdant green, yellow and rouge and the kind of orange that could forever warm me to the depths of my bones. Black and white? No. Color. Ones I'd never seen.

Along the arc of the path, in the distance just over the tops of the flowers, there was a little blue pompom of hair. I could just see it, just around the bend.

And there were others, too.

My family.

I saw now, where the house of Kreios should have been up on the high cliffs, only a waterfall and the eagle's nest I remembered. The mother eagle was perched above, watching her baby, now a little older, now a little more experienced.

He had learned to fly. His cry pierced the skies.

A Preview of

The 'Naturals

A Young Adult Supernatural Science Fiction Serial

CHAPTER ONE: ISRAEL

IT WASN'T THAT HE hated his life; it was just that he hated who
he was. He wanted to be stronger, stand up for himself but never
found the courage to do anything besides take it like a punching
bag. Scrap that, his life sucked.

Israel James sat hunched over in the back of the lame minivan,
Foster the People cranked through his ear buds. Trees whisked by.
His eyes got heavy. How long would this move last? A year, two?
Did it matter? The idea of a normal life, whatever that was, flew out
the window like so much air.

His little sister, Molly, was asleep, her head bobbing from side
to side as they navigated through the mountains. Her hands still
had a firm grip on an advanced calculus book, as if passing him
academically was all-important to her.

His dad caught his eye in the rearview mirror. "Almost there,
sport," Israel turned up the music and clenched his fists.

They'd been on the road for eight hours and all he wanted was
to get out, move a little and breathe some fresh air.

Israel eyed his father. It was as if he was a robot or something.

It was all a show, the appearance of kindness and normalcy. Israel first started to notice the change when he was 4. His best friend Frank Douglas would have have him over for sleepovers all the time and watching Frank's parents interact with each other was so different then what Israel was used too.

Israel missed Frank and his other friends. This move, the new town all represented more of the same. What am I supposed to do? Make more fake friends and get comfortable just to have to move again? He probably wouldn't even get to finish high school before he'd have to move for the fifteenth time.

High School, that was a joke. He was the home-schooled reject, the odd guy in every town they had ever lived in. His mom didn't really teach him, he had to do it on his own. She didn't have the patience for it, and why they wouldn't let him go to a normal school made no sense.

Something flashed in the woods just beyond the tree line and for a second Israel swore it was a bear, yet it had a metallic silver color. His heart pounded in his chest so fast that he actually gasped.

"Dad, stop!" Israel ripped his ear buds out and grabbed the back of his moms seat.

"We're almost there son, hold it till we get into town." His voice was calm and low, his 'don't push it' voice.

He didn't know why but he had to get out, needed to follow that thing he'd seen. "I have to stop… I'm gonna be sick! NOW!"

He was yelling, he never yelled, never so much as raised his voice, he was the quiet brooding type. His face tingled and he flexed his legs, it was getting hard to breathe.

"Okay, okay, just don't throw up in the car. Roll your window down if you can't make it," his dad said. He threw him an irritated look.

Israel stuck his face out the window as the minivan slowed and his dad pulled off the main road into a small dirt cutout. There it was again, a flash of silver in the trees, slowing as if following the car.

Before the van came to a full stop Israel sprang out and ran toward the woods.

Legs pumping, he could hear his mom calling after him. He didn't care, it was nothing, he was nothing, it was—

Branches slapped his body and face. He tripped on something and went down hard. Dirt and rocks dug into his hands sending pain up his arms. He clawed at the ground and got to his feet. The wooded area opened up and a clearing of grass and wild flowers stretched in front of him. It was breathtaking, but something wasn't right. This was not right, the woods, the trees, his beating heart and dry mouth.

Smelling the air, he waited. He didn't know why, but he did. Breathing in the scent of pine trees and wet earth, he turned at the sight of movement a hundred yards or so, just north of the clearing.

A warm stream of urine ran down his legs as he stared at … what?

There were no words.

Knees weak, he fell to the ground shaking. Sobbing he wiped at his eyes trying to see through his tears. He didn't know what to do. There was a force, calling him somehow as if they were connected. He liked it yet a part of him feared what it meant.

It turned and looked at him, eyes like glass. The monster stood well over ten feet tall and almost as wide, yet it moved so fast, so smooth. Like nothing he'd seen on earth before. Did it have fur? His mind ran through the possibilities but came up short, how could something so machine like have fur? All he wanted to do was run, to cry in his mother's arms and find comfort, but he couldn't look away.

Then, it vanished.

Wiping his eyes again, he scanned the clearing.

Nothing.

Had he imagined it? His gut told him no but where had it gone?

The connection broke. Israel stood to his feet. He stumbled backward; the ground was black, charred and smoking. Was there a fire, why didn't he feel it?

He was standing in the middle of some sort of blast area. His hands were warm and he turned them over to find that his palms were black as well. They didn't hurt but the skin blistered and to his amazement the white flesh began to flake away and—heal.

"Almost here! Are you kids excited?" He looked up from his burnt hands at his father's eyes peering at him in the rearview mirror of the minivan. How did he get back here? His arms were unscathed, his pants dry.

Was he dreaming? Burping he held back the bile that wanted to come up. It was happening again, just like last time.

So what was going on with him? He was living these things, and they were real. Sort of. There was no proof. This last one really shook him up, his palms still had black smudges and he could remember parts of it.? How much was real and how much was all in his head? He remembered four other times he had an *incident*, it was not something he could forget.

"We're thinking of letting you guys take a few classes in school this year, just to get you out more, you know, have a social life."

Foster the People blared in his ears and he wiped a bead of sweat from his forehead. Searching the woods as they flew by his window, he could feel a tug, something calling him. This time he would not stuff it under, he needed to find out what was wrong with him.

***

"WHAT IS WRONG WITH me?" Israel muttered as they pulled into town.

"Where should I start? Neurotic, mean, ugly, and a complete bore." Molly crossed her arms and gave him her signature grin, the one that said, 'you're beneath me in so many ways.'

"I wasn't talking to you, just thinking out loud."

"Thinking? Really, did it hurt?" Molly chuckled and Israel contemplated punching her in the arm.

Molly was younger then him by two years, but at 15 she was uber smart. And annoying. Her scores on state tests were off the charts and she was all but graduated. Israel didn't like her much, well that wasn't true. He loved her because she was his sister, but she was a punk.

"Whatever Molly." Nice, a brilliant comeback.

They pulled into the gas station and Israel unbuckled.

"No junk food you two. Think about your bodies," his mom called after him. Molly rolled her eyes as she rounded the front of the mini van. She was tall for her age and showed signs of the change. Blonde and full of spunk, she always had boys flocking to her as if she were made of candy or something. Israel hunched over and pulled his hoodie up and followed Molly into the Chevron.

"Think about your bodies," Molly mocked. "Really Issi, she's like the food Nazi. I hate hiding food in my room like a prisoner. A girl just needs some chocolate every now and then."

"Yeah, well, you know how she is … I don't think she is gonna change any time soon."

"Did you know that she made me eat this nasty barley stuff the other day? She said it would help my cramps."

"Ugh, Molly, gross, come on!"

"It's true."

Israel turned up his iPod and walked down the candy isle.

Grabbing a Snickers and a bag of mixed nuts. He paid and shoved the Snickers into his pocket, making sure to toss the receipt in the trash on the way out.

Climbing into the back seat he held up the bag of mixed nuts and his mom nodded approvingly.

Molly took forever as usual. Dad pumped gas and Israel closed his eyes and tossed a handful of nuts into his mouth. The blackouts, visions or whatever they were worried him, did he have a tumor or something?

His father sighed as he got into the van. "Gas prices are out of control. 98 bucks to fill up, 98 bucks!"

"Yes well, it's all part of what we must pay to enjoy this great country. You should be glad we have a car and you got a new job." His mother patted him on the arm.

Here they went again, it was their fake 'we love everyone and never get stressed out about anything' attitudes. Israel groaned and reached in his pocket, grabbing the Snickers bar.

"You're right dear, its a small price to pay for what we have, we're truly blessed."

Gag.

"Hey Issi, you looking forward to taking a few classes at school this year, maybe make some new friends?"

"Um, yeah, sure." He wanted a good friend like Frank, wanted it badly but he would never let his parents know that.

"Now Son, you sound like you're not excited about this. Just think--new house, new friends, new experience, it'll be great!"

"Sure Dad … Just tired, I'm excited—really!" It was all he could do to fake it, but he'd learned from the best.

***

THEIR NEW HOUSE WAS just OK. As expected. It was in the Waterford District, whatever that was. It was in the poor side of town. Most the houses were older and rundown.

"I thought you were gonna make more money?" Molly said what everyone else was thinking but didn't have the nerve to say out loud.

"I am making a lot more money, but we can fix this house up and make it our own. It will be a great character building project."

"Great," Molly muttered.

"What was that dear?" Mom said with a threatening smile.

"Nothing,"

"This is a great house." Mom said. "It's older, yes, but just think, you can make your rooms just the way you want them."

Israel watched this exchange with some amusement. Molly should have known better then to expect something nice. It was not the James family style.

"Can we go in?" Israel said.

"Sure thing, sport. Go on in and pick out your new room."

"Thanks dad."

Israel made his way up the broken porch and into the damp smelling house. It was rather large and had a wide staircase leading up to a second floor. The paint on the walls was peeling and Israel guessed the place was over one hundred years old.

"This house is like the haunted mansion from a movie," Molly groaned and looked around in disgust. "Mom, come on ... we can't live here, this place should be condemned!"

"Molly dear, it'll be great, just you wait and see. Now be a good girl and go pick out your room, there are plenty to choose from." Her tone dropped and Molly caught on to the inflection.

The house was huge. Israel counted six rooms. He found his as soon as he walked though the doorway. It was large, and had a window with a window seat overlooking the street, and a side window that looked out over the neighbor's yard.

There was no door but he could fix that. He'd lived in places like this his whole life.

Tossing his backpack onto the window seat he opened the door to a walk-in closet. This was perfect. He would never admit it to his parents, but this place rocked. It was old, creepy, had lots of rooms, and Israel was sure it held some secrets. He would make it his mission to discover all of them.

"Found one you like?"

Israel jumped as his dad's overly-chipper voice.

"Uh … yeah."

"Good. I'll figure out something to give you some privacy. Can't have a cool pad without a door," Dad said.

Molly walked by the open doorway and thrust her head forward and shuffled her feet as is she were being dragged to her death.

"Come on Molly, it's not that bad. Pick a room and help me get the van unloaded."

Once he was alone again Israel munched on the rest of his Snickers bar and sat with his legs up in the window seat and checked out the house next door. They had one of the nice houses on the street and even had a pool.

He watched a girl swim laps and about choked when she got out. She was in a bikini and was tall with dark nearly black hair. Ducking down he watched her pick up a book and lay down on a towel.

Things were looking up, cool old house, hottie next door and his sister was miserable. Maybe this move wouldn't be so bad after all.

***

"ISSI, MOLLY, DINNER."

Israel stared up at the cracked ceiling and let the room have him. He dozed off and must have been really out as most of his clothes were unpacked and folded neatly on the floor in front of his dresser.

The moving van showed up an hour after they arrived and the movers emptied the van and he was left to put his bed together. Israel didn't have much furniture to speak of, a bed, dresser and a writing desk. He liked to write, short stories and maybe one day a novel.

"Dinner." Her voice was sharper and Israel rolled out of his bed and took the stairs two at a time. Everyone was already seated and at once he knew something was wring. Molly sat all stiff and mom and dad were extra chipper.

"Have a seat son." Dad waved a hand to a chair across from Molly.

Heat burned his palms and the feeling was almost pleasant. Sitting down he waited.

"I went ahead and ordered us a pizza, I know, I know, it is so bad for you but I wanted to make this day special." Molly had her head down and would not look at him. Something was definitely up.

The smell of pepperoni and hot cheese made Israel's mouth water. Dad opened the large pizza box with a Garbanzo's Pizza label on the lid. He placed a large slice on Molly's plate and one on his and moms. Shutting the lid Israel looked up at what his mom was holding out to him.

"Here you go dear," She handed him an empty Snickers wrapper and a fork.

Stunned Israel just stared at the wrapper unable to move. Mom leaned over and placed the Snickers wrapper on his plate and slid the fork next to his plate.

"So, big day tomorrow. Molly, you and I should go shopping, pick out some cool stuff for your new room." Molly nodded and stared at her pizza, hair hanging over her face.

Dad took a huge bite and grinned. "Wow, this is amazing, I didn't know how hungry I was till I took a bite."

The Snickers bar wrapper lay there as if mocking him. Warm heat flared in his neck and arms. Keeping calm he looked up and smiled. "I know what you mean dad, so hungry." Taking the wrapper he crumpled it up and shoved it into his mouth.

He somehow managed to get it down and Molly finally looked up and smiled at him. It was not a cruel smile but one of knowing. They were in this together and no matter how they felt about each other they would always have each other's back.

***

"ISRAEL JAMES, THAT'S A different name, are your parents religious?"

Israel sat on the edge of the examination table and shivered. "Sorta, but not really. I think they were being weird just to be weird."

Doctor Bradshaw laughed. It was a good laugh, deep and pronounced. "Well, I guess that is as good a reason as any." The big man placed the cold, no freezing stethoscope on his bare chest and Israel breathed in deep. He knew the drill.

"What do you think of Silverwood so far? Make any new friends?"

"Not yet just got in yesterday." The paper on the table crackled and Israel tried not to move so much, it was annoying.

"I think you will like it, we got a good thing going here. I grew up here and even played football for the Silverwood Heralds, that may mean nothing to you now but they took state every year I played. Now…not so much."

"You play quarterback?"

"Linebacker,"

"Nice,"

"I went over your charts that your other doctor sent over. You have quite a history," Dr. Bradshaw looked over his glasses at Israel and half smiled. "Do you know what you have, I mean to say, do you understand what it is?"

"I think so, there is some fancy word for it but the short story is my blood is to thick, I make to much or something, so I have to get bleed every three months or so."

"That's about right."

"I've had it all my life so it's no biggie, just have to remember to go in."

"Have you had any shortness of breath or loss of energy?"

"Nope, sometimes I get overheated but my last doctor said that was normal for my condition."

Doctor Bradshaw rolled back and looked Israel up and down. "I am a little concerned, your bone mass is not where it should be, and by the look of your skin you are lacking is some key nutrition. Are you eating enough?"

The cold steel under his feet and the lack of clothing gave him the chills but he was not cold now. Warmness crawled up his arm and Israel began to sweat.

"Enough, but my mom harps on me to eat better, I like sugar and soda."

Dr. Bradshaw nodded and wrote something in his chart. "I am going to put you on a prenatal supplement. I put pregnant mothers on this as a way to get extra nutrition, Now, now, don't worry, it s not a drug or something just for girls. It is a really strong multi vitamin. You need to take one with each meal or three times a day, just make sure you eat something with it as it can give you a gut ache."

"That it?"

"Yes, the nurse will come in and take some blood, you can get dressed if you like, we have a more comfortable chair in the other room. Have you eaten today?"

"Yes." Israel lied.

"Good. It was good to meet you, I want to run some tests on your blood to confirm a few questions I have, but aside from the results I'll see you in three months."

"Thanks."

Israel lay back on the table after dressing and took a deep breath in and let it out slowly. Drawing up his hands he stared at his palms. They looked normal yet he could feel the warmth. What was going on?

Read the rest of The 'Naturals, available now.

A Preview of USA Today Bestseller

SWEET DREAMS

Book 1 in the WJA series
A Mark Appleton Thriller

CHAPTER ONE

JULY. TEHRAN, IRAN. IT wasn't just hot. It was hell. The heat
would melt shoes to the pavement if a person stood in one place
too long. The night air should bring some relief with its cool, musty
smell of sand and sweat. However, it seemed this evening the
cooling desert would not give up any of its pride and send a much-
needed breeze into the city. No, this night was muggy, sticky, and
just plain miserable.

Despite the heat, tonight was like any other night for
Hokamend. Seated on a pillow in his private quarters, he was
reading, like he did every night. This evening, the book was *The
Fall of America.*

He and his best friend, who'd been killed in a bus bombing
six years earlier, had spent countless hours together going over the
plans and drawings of the Chicago metro system, trying to find the
perfect place to set off the explosive.

Muttering a prayer to Allah for success, he looked through the
open window at the sky and noticed it was devoid of stars. A storm

was moving in to tease them with the possibility of sweet relief from the godforsaken heat. But he knew in the end the cloud would leave without so much as a drop of rain.

He envied his friend, who was in a place beyond this world, a place he could only dream of. He turned back to his book, reminding himself of all the work yet to be done. Someone had to complete the job, someone had to finish off those arrogant Americans.

His hatred for America and disdain for the people who infested the land made him want to spit. He pictured their smug faces and fancy cars. He would bring the infidels to their knees. He would wake the sleeping giant, then rip its head off.

A bodyguard walked past his door. He heard footsteps and it jolted him out of his daydream. His guards were the best that money could buy. They walked in four shifts and in different patterns every hour to keep lurking enemies confused. Hokamend was a careful man. He never took chances with his own life. True, he demanded his followers to give up their lives in service to Allah, but he was different. With a half-million-dollar American government bounty on his head, he was worth more, much more.

On the other hand, such a reward for betrayal could cause even friends to consider the offer. But he was no fool. Chopped off fingers, toes, and even a tongue now and then had a way of driving the truth home—under no circumstances should one cross Hokamend.

He slipped to his feet and walked to the double French doors leading out to a balcony, lighting up a cigar.

He touched the small scar above his right eye and smelled the cigar. "A battle wound," he would say. He was proud of his many scars. They proved his devotion to Allah. They proved he was not just an administrator but that he'd fought in the battles.

A small flicker flashed against the night sky as he struck the lighter and drew on his hand-rolled Cuban. He scanned his property, searching for snipers or anything that might be out of place but found nothing amiss, which didn't surprise him. After all, this was the perfect location for his palace. Situated at the apex of a hill, the mansion was surrounded by a high wall with guard towers at each corner manned by armed snipers. Beyond the wall, two chain-link fences made a wide circle around the perimeter of the grounds. Razor wire coiled across the tops of both fences, and fifteen highly trained guard dogs roamed in between. If someone were to make it past the first fence and was lucky enough to avoid the dogs, then the snipers would ensure he didn't see another sunrise.

An open lawn devoid of obstructions surrounded the palace in a one-mile circle. Deliberately designed so an enemy could not hide behind anything, the grounds looked more like a park than a secure compound.

He watched the city lights in the distance twinkle and blink like little bat eyes staring back at him, trying to ascertain if he was friend or foe. He took a deep draw, let out a cloud of thick smoke and wondered when they would figure it out, if ever. *No, they don't have the stomach for it. They are weak.*

A mosquito landed on his arm and started sucking blood like a miniature vampire. He swatted at the pest but missed as it dodged just in time to save its worthless life. "Stupid bugs," he muttered. They were out in force tonight, and there was no cool breeze to fend them off.

The mosquito buzzed by him again. He swung his hand at it and cursed. This time, he made contact with the bloodsucker, spreading a red smear across his arm.

He swore again. The nasty pests were ruining his quiet time. With his busy life, he treasured this hour of the day when he could think and clear his head, not to mention enjoy a good cigar.

He felt another prick on the side of his neck. More like a bee sting than a mosquito bite, this one hurt. He rubbed his neck but didn't feel anything unusual. In fact, he didn't feel anything. Nothing at all. His fingers were numb, like hard rubber chafing against his neck. A cold shiver ran up his spine. It was as if someone else was touching him. He had sensation in the rest of his body, but his hands were dead.

The bite began to throb, and a terrible heat burned through his body. He stumbled back into his study, drenched in sweat.

Screaming, he fell to the floor, clutching his head with unfeeling fingers. He dug his nails into his skull as if that would make the pain stop.

He yelled for a guard—anyone—to help him, but no one came to his aid.

The pain sharpened. His ears rang with a deafening sound like the air horns he'd heard as a boy just before a bomb exploded and more people died. Writhing on the floor, he shouted again for help. Then reality hit. No sound came out of his mouth. Just air.

Every nerve in his body flashed with impossible heat. Curled in a ball on the floor, he grasped his ears, trying to stop the noise that pounded against his skull.

Something was wrong with his ear. He pulled a hand away and blinked, not believing what he saw. Plastered in his palm, his right ear sizzled like a piece of hot bacon. He tried to focus, to make his brain work. But he couldn't think. The pain was beyond maddening. Mouthing a curse, he crushed the bloody ear in his hand as pain swept through his body like a wave of molten lava. The agony was so sharp and excruciating all he could do was writhe on the floor, clawing at his head and face.

Outside his door, his bodyguards took wagers as to which one he would curse tonight for not getting him his drink on time.

**

MARK APPLETON QUIETLY MADE his way down from his rooftop perch, where he had just carried out another flawless hit. No one seemed to be aware of his presence, which was the way he liked it. Hokamend's guards wouldn't discover his body until the next morning. Most guards for hire these days were lazy alcoholics.

He'd hidden his blond hair under a dark baseball cap that matched the rest of his attire: black cargo pants, a long-sleeved black shirt with patches on the elbows and a tiny pocket on the left arm for his throwing knife, and black boots. His hands were covered in dark, lambskin gloves, which fit like a second skin. He silently slipped across the rooftop to a zip line, his access to this particular building.

Made of a small, woven cable used in airplane wings and developed by NASA, the eighth-inch line could support as much as three-thousand pounds. Using a high-powered yet small crossbow, he shot a tiny anchor at an adjacent building five hundred yards away. Once the anchor penetrated the brick it would spread to form a solid hold.

He slung his weapon over his shoulder, hooked himself to the line, and started his soundless descent to the shorter building. A door on the rooftop led to a back stairway. He crept through the abandoned building, which was empty except for a homeless drunk here and there. He wrinkled his nose. The smell of urine and mold made even the musty air outside seem like a fresh ocean breeze. He made sure he didn't wake any of the drunks as he traversed the twelve flights of stairs.

Once he was on the main level he made a right through a broken, wooden door into an empty room. Half of the wallpaper was torn off the walls and the carpet was long gone, leaving warped plywood behind. This part of town reminded him of tornado country. Some buildings were beautiful and untouched by the bombs. Others were about to cave in on themselves. War had a way of leaving its mark on more than just the people.

He quickly disassembled his weapon, and as he did so, searched the room for anything he might have left or any sign that could tie him to the dilapidated building. He folded the gun in half where the black barrel and plastic stock met. The scope snapped off with a soft click. His weapon of choice was custom made and could fire a paper round up to three miles, if the wind was right. He shoved the gun pieces in a backpack and hefted it onto his shoulder. Once everything was secure, he pulled a small remote from his pocket and stepped outside, where he peered around the corner, made sure no one spotted him, and pushed the button.

He could hear a faint sizzling sound as the zip line above him melted, then turned to ash and floated down in small flakes. Good, no trace. He ran across the street and walked three blocks south.

Tehran, like most cities in the desert, came alive after nightfall. People smoked outside the bars and griped about the heat. He could hear laughter from inside one bar he passed. Outside another he heard a thump, like someone falling off a chair, then the sound of glass shattering.

The streets were made of concrete and asphalt. Some intersections were lined with cobblestones. A multitude of blinking lights over storefronts strived to draw traffic to look at their wares. He made his way down a back alley, keeping his head down and avoiding eye contact. All he wanted was to get back to his place and get some sleep.

He stopped at a one-story shop with graffiti sprayed alongside the faded front door. A Persian sign above the door read *Sporting Goods*. The brick building wasn't much to look at with thick, black steel bars embedded in the wooden front door. The boarded-up windows also had the local kids' handiwork spray painted on them.

He inserted a key. The lock clicked. Using another key, he released the deadbolt. The heavy door creaked as he pushed it open and stepped inside. Pulling off his ball cap, he tossed it on the coat rack.

The shop was an open room with two rows of metal shelves in the middle stocked with a complete line of camping supplies: Coleman stoves and dehydrated foods ranging from stew to peach cobbler. Or for the old-school type, he could buy the original MREs and hope his taste buds were on vacation. The racks against the walls went all the way around the room and came to a stop at the front desk, which was topped by a cash register and a glass case containing pistols and knives. Behind the counter, guns of every shape and size, from shotguns to M16s, were racked from floor to ceiling. All of them had been previously owned but were in good working order.

The shop was not much, but it was clean, and it provided a good place for him to hide as he researched his target. The owner was a native who worked for the same organization he did. As far as anyone else was concerned, Mark was an out-of-town guest.

He stepped to the back of the little shop and stopped in front of a shelf full of books on how to fish and hunt and stay alive in the desert. He ran his fingers along the back of the books. When he located the fingertip-size button, he pushed it and a deep, groaning sound sliced the silence. The floor on his right split in the middle and opened up to reveal a concrete staircase. The hole was six-by-six and the concrete lid opened downward and hung like bomb bay doors on a plane. He started down and the floor closed above him with a solid thud. Wall lights flickered and came to life. At the bottom of the stairs, he stopped before a metal door with oversized rivets and bolts around the edges. A small, red light behind a glass bubble protruding from the wall glowed like an evil eye.

He placed his hand on the LCD screen mounted to the right of the door. The screen lit up and ran a scan of his handprint. He leaned down and spoke into a box, making sure to pronounce each syllable perfectly. "Appleton, Mark."

The red sensor above the door hummed as a red laser shot out and fanned at the end. Beginning at the top of his head, it scanned down his body, taking readings of his frame and measurements of each bone like an X-ray, though much more advanced. The light turned green when the scan was finished and the door unlocked and slid down into the floor.

What lay beyond was not a concrete bunker or a dingy underground hideout. Instead, it was a house. Not a real house, but it was as much of a house as one could get this far away from home. The first room looked like a typical American living room, minus the picture window. To the right was a kitchen with a black refrigerator, stove, and a microwave oven. To the left was a sitting area with a fireplace and a fifty-inch, surround-sound plasma screen television and a Blu-ray player. A couch with big, fluffy cushions faced the TV, and a camelhair rug graced the floor.

He punched a code on a keypad mounted on the wall on the far side of the living room, and a hidden door opened. The whooshing sound it made always reminded him of a Star Trek movie. Lights inside the room flashed on to reveal case after case of weapons and ammunition. He unpacked his backpack on a metal table that stood against a wall near the front of the weapons room. After he cleaned and oiled his gun, he placed it in an eight-foot glass case next to a Glock. Every wall supported similar cases containing guns, C4 explosives, landmines, and rocket launchers. Most of the weapons and ammo boasted his personal touches, from bullets made of paper to guns powered by air and sound waves.

At his touch the door whooshed back into place and blended into the wall as if it never existed. He stretched, pulled off his shirt, and ran his fingers through his hair. He craved a cool shower and a shave. The stakeout and events leading up to the kill had taken a year of stalking and many long, boring nights waiting for a clear shot.

The cool water felt good as it cascaded over his lean body and washed away the stress of the day.

He thought about the terrorist he'd just killed. He knew he should be sad or feel a little guilty about killing another man, but he couldn't bring himself to even feel bad. Because of all the things Hokamend had done—the bombings of schools and playgrounds that had killed and maimed dozens of children, and the snipers who shot twenty-plus people at a time in major American cities before anyone realized a massacre was in progress.

He turned off the water, thinking, *It's time for the terrorists of the world to live in fear instead of us fearing them.* After he shaved, he grabbed a pair of shorts from the dresser in his bedroom and slipped them on. Much better. Nothing like a comfortable pair of shorts.

In the kitchen, he pulled a dinner from the freezer and zapped it in the microwave. He turned the package over and saw that this dinner offered a tasty slab of chicken with mashed potatoes and a brownie to boot.

He chuckled. K certainly wouldn't approve. A microwave dinner and a soda? He could hear her exclaim, "Not healthy!" and see his wife's playful frown.

The smell of fake chicken filled the kitchen. He was too tired to cook tonight. Plus, he hadn't had a chance to restock his refrigerator. He sat down on the leather couch and began to eat.

Not bad, for a TV dinner. Not like K's cooking, though. Not much like anybody's cooking.

Now that he was on the subject, he couldn't help but think about K and his daughter, Samantha. It had been three years since… he shook his head, trying to shove the thought from his brain. *Wow. Three years. Time flies.*

Finished, he got up and threw the empty container in the trash, feeling a little celebratory. He was done with the mission and that meant only one thing.

Vacation—after a good night's sleep.

He turned off the lights and his alarm clock and crawled into his king-size bed. He was going to sleep in, which would be a nice change from the multiple all-nighters he'd pulled in the last year. He closed his eyes and drew the covers around his chin. No matter how hot it was outside, he had to be under the covers.

Once he had breathed in deep and let it all out in a long sigh, he relaxed his legs and arms. His eyes became heavy. Thoughts of his family consumed his mind until he fell asleep, which usually took a couple hours, but tonight he had a feeling he would fall asleep right away. He wished he could see K and her sparkling hazel eyes and the smile she reserved for him and him alone.

Then there was little Samantha, with her cute pigtails bobbing as she ran down the steps to meet him. The workday tensions melted when he felt her tiny arms hugging his neck. She always smelled like soap and lavender, no matter how dirty she was or how long she'd gone between baths. It seemed like just yesterday he was home holding K and Samantha in his arms. He hated to go to bed alone, again. So alone.

Three years earlier…

Read the rest of Sweet Dreams, available now.

ABOUT THE AUTHORS

Aaron Patterson

AARON PATTERSON IS THE father of three kids: Soleil, Kale, and Klayton. He is the New York Times and USA Today bestselling author of The Mark Appleton thriller series, The Airel Saga, and The Sarah Steele thriller series. He worked in the construction field for 11 years and is now a full time writer. He was home schooled and has a bachelor's degree in theology. He loves to hike, snowboard, camp, and drink coconut lattes. He is also the founder of StoneHouse Ink and co-founder of StoneHouse University. He speaks all over the country on the subjects of eBooks, writing, and the changing publishing world.

Connect with Aaron at his blog: http://theworstbookever. blogspot.com

Friend him on Facebook: www.facebook.com/aaronpatterson

And follow him on Twitter: @mstersmith

Sign up for Aaron's newsletter for updates on his new books, and way cool deals including free eBooks. You will not get bugged with a ton of emails, you'll get a message only when he has something awesome to announce or give away. Sign up here: http://eepurl.com/tQWHb

Chris White

YOU KNOW WHAT THEY say—that behind every great man is an unstoppable rebel force—and it's true. Like Moriarty was to Holmes, C.P. White is the reversed polarity doppelganger behind it all. He blogs about weirdness on the C.P. White Media Blog and spins dark tales, psychological thrillers that you'll want to read with the lights on. He works in the front office writing romantic YA paranormal fiction with Aaron Patterson, collaborates with illustrator Joey Zavaleta on the Great Jammy Adventure children's books, and even plays sometime editor to his award-winning author friends. Both personalities will fight to the death for a bowl of high quality mac-n-cheese. C.P. doesn't mind living with spiders, but only because his house is old and they were there first. He prefers riding bikes and playing nice, he dislikes boring people on general principle, and is apt to launch bottle rockets through open windows. Both agree that their least favorite thing is dog exhaust on the bottom of their shoe. You can learn more about author Chris White, as well as author C.P. White, at http://www.cpwhitemedia.com.

MORGANTOWN PUBLIC LIBRARY
373 SPRUCE STREET
MORGANTOWN, WV 26505

CPSIA information can be obtained
at www.ICGtesting.com
Printed in the USA
LVOW03s1219160717
541557LV00001B/183/P